BEAR IN A BOOKSHOP

BODYGUARD SHIFTERS #3

ZOE CHANT

Bear in a Bookshop

Author's Note

This book stands alone and contains a complete HEA romance. However, if you'd like to read the other books in the Bodyguard Shifters series, here's the series so far, in order:

And don't miss the spinoff series, Stone Shifters:

You may also enjoy Bodyguard Shifters Collection 1, collecting books 1-4.

GUNNAR

"Hey, Sorenson," the guard called. "You got a visitor."

Gunnar Sorenson swiped his mop across the floor one last time and leaned it neatly against the wall. He didn't have a lot of things to be proud of these days, but he was proud of this floor. It practically gleamed.

His ma always used to say if a job was worth doing, it was worth doing well.

... For all the good that advice had done him in life. Good thing she wasn't around to see him now.

"Sorenson." The guard's voice had a hard edge. "Today?" He jangled his cuffs meaningfully.

Gunnar smoothed down his orange coverall, held out his hands, and submitted wordlessly to being cuffed. Inside his chest, his bear snarled and paced.

We could break those flimsy things. We could be free!

Yeah, he thought back. *Free to do what? Free to be fugitives, that's what.*

We didn't do anything wrong! his bear growled.

Gunnar didn't answer. He'd tried to explain it to his bear, and he didn't feel like going through another round of their

1

mutual failure to understand each other. Especially since, deep down inside, he agreed with his bear. He hadn't done anything wrong. Not morally wrong.

The trouble was, the law didn't see it that way.

So even though he could have broken the handcuffs, unleashed the enormous bear inside him, and made a break for it, he let the guard lead him out of the cell block.

A rattling noise made him look up. Here came good old "Hammer" Jones, on library duty today, pushing the book-cart. The other inmate nodded to him; Gunnar nodded back. He couldn't help himself; his eyes followed the bookcart wistfully. He wasn't the kind of guy who got library duty, though. Dropped out of school in the eighth grade and could barely read above a fourth-grade level—might as well face it, books and libraries weren't meant for guys like him.

"Eyes forward, Sorenson," the guard told him, and waited until he complied before unlocking the door that led out of the cell block to the visiting room.

With the bookcart out of sight, there was nothing to distract Gunnar and stop him from wondering who was here to see him. There wasn't anybody he could think of. In the three years he'd been here, he hadn't gotten a single visitor.

Not even Nils, who was the entire reason he was here.

Not for the first time (or the hundredth, or the thousandth) Gunnar pushed down thoughts of his brother. Nils was ... Nils. Nothing Gunnar did could have changed him, or helped him.

Even though he'd tried.

And he really doubted Nils was his visitor today. Nils wouldn't be caught dead coming inside a prison of his own free will. Not even to visit his little brother. *Especially* not to visit his little brother.

The guard opened the door to the visiting room. It was a plain, bare room, with tables and chairs bolted to the concrete floor. A few other inmates were in there already, mostly guys visiting with their wives and girlfriends. Gunnar averted his eyes, wanting to give them privacy, and scanned over the tables looking for who might be here to see him.

There was only one table with a visitor sitting alone, not already talking to someone. Gunnar had never seen this man before in his life, but as Gunnar's eyes met the stranger's, a sharp look of shock and recognition passed over the other man's face, and he stood up. Gunnar dropped his gaze and tried to study the other guy from the corner of his eye as the guard led him toward the table. One thing prison had given him was a well-developed ability to look at people without appearing to look at them.

The stranger was dark-haired and lean, though not slight by any means. He was shorter than Gunnar but looked like he could handle himself in a fight. Gunnar couldn't figure out what kind of person he was. He wasn't dressed up enough to be a lawyer, but he wasn't dressed *down* enough to be the sort of guy who typically came in here to visit a buddy; he wore a black button-down shirt and black jeans. His eyes were his most striking feature—light gray, piercing, and intense.

Gunnar's bear, already restless, bristled at that pale, probing stare. Gunnar pushed it down.

"Gunnar Sorenson?" the stranger asked.

Gunnar nodded.

"Sit," the guard told Gunnar. He sat, and the guard locked his handcuffs to a ring under the edge of the table. "Five minutes," the guard said, and left them alone.

"I'd shake hands," Gunnar said. He shrugged and rattled his cuffs. "But ..."

"Don't worry about it." The stranger had seated himself again. He didn't look either hostile or afraid of Gunnar; he just seemed wary. "Do you know who I am?"

3

"Not a clue," Gunnar said.

"My name is Deputy Ben Keegan. I used to be a big-city cop; now I'm with the sheriff's department in a town called Autumn Grove. And there's something I need your help with."

"You need my help, huh?" Gunnar couldn't stop himself; he gave a short laugh. "Yeah, sure, what the hell, Deputy. What can I help you with today?"

"You have a brother named Nils, right?" All the humor fell straight out of Gunnar's world, and the bottom dropped out of his stomach. When Gunnar didn't answer, Keegan gave him a brief, fierce smile. "Of course you do. You're the spitting image of him. What are you, twins?"

"He's four years older," Gunnar said. His throat felt tight. He imagined himself as this cop must see him: huge, muscular, tattooed, his blond hair cropped close to his scalp.

He knew he looked like a killer, even though he'd never harmed another person in his life.

"Has your brother been in touch with you since you've been in prison?" Keegan asked.

The tightness in his throat and chest increased, along with the sense of the walls closing in on him. "No," Gunnar said simply.

Keegan leaned back in his chair and regarded him. "Not even once. Not once in three years."

"You come here to rub it in or what?" Gunnar's voice came out harsh. He told himself it didn't hurt. Not anymore.

But it still did.

"Your brother escaped from prison," Keegan said. "Six weeks ago."

Gunnar felt like he'd been punched in the gut. He hadn't even known Nils was in prison in the first place. When Gunnar had gone inside, he hadn't been.

"You didn't know that?" Keegan asked, and Gunnar shook

his head. "Well, there's more. He's gone to ground and no one knows where he is, but I'm worried he's going to come after some people I care about. People who helped put him away the first time. So I'm here to cut you a deal, Gunnar. I'll get you out of prison, if you help me catch your brother."

MELODY

"**M**elody, you have to listen to me!"

"I'm *listening*," Melody Keegan said impatiently, moving on to the Philosophy shelf to tuck a book back into its proper place between its neighbors. Oh no, what was this one doing here? That was entirely out of place—it belonged in Mystery.

"No, you're not," Tessa protested, following her. "You're—you're—you're *shelving*!"

With a sigh, balancing the never-shrinking, ever-growing stack of books in her arms, Melody turned and looked at her longtime best friend and, now, sister-in-law. Tessa had grown her short hair out over the last year, and now a riot of dark brown curls surrounded a face that was softer than it had been when Melody had first met her ... in more ways than one. Pregnancy was a good look on her. She was rounded and softened all over, and looked vastly less emotionally guarded, less unhappy, than she had been for most of the time that Melody had known her.

Being married to Melody's brother Ben was good for her.

And Melody loved having Tessa for a neighbor and for a sister.

However ...

"You don't have to worry about me," Melody said, and couldn't help smiling. With her hands full of books, she used an elbow to shove her glasses up her nose. "This feels like a turnaround, doesn't it?"

"What?" Tessa said, her train of thought visibly derailing.

"The entire reason why you met my brother and ended up married to him is because I sprang him on you as a surprise bodyguard." Melody shook her head as she moved on to tuck a dog-eared Dick Francis paperback and a nice first-edition Agatha Christie back onto their respective shelves in the Mystery section of the store. "I remember how you argued about it, insisted you could handle it yourself."

"Yes, and you know what, as it turned out, you were right. I really was in danger, and I couldn't handle it myself. And now you need to learn from my mistakes, and just come with me, where you'll be safe, and Ben and Derek can protect you!"

"Tessa ... there's a key difference between you and me." Melody rearranged the order of several Sue Grafton alphabet mysteries as she spoke. There was nothing worse than an alphabet out of order. As she fixed the shelf, a clatter came from the direction of the bookstore's small café, making her wince.

"And what would that be?" Tessa demanded, planting her hands on hips that had always been generous, but pregnancy had pushed in the direction of "ample."

"You *know* what." Melody cut her eyes sideways at the café, where her one part-time employee was fumbling with the espresso machine, and leaned close to whisper, "I'm a dragon, Tessa. I can take care of myself."

7

"Miss Keegan?" came a plaintive call from behind the machine. "Miss Keegan, I think I broke something."

Melody could feel one of her eyes twitching. "Broken on the machine or on you, Jimmy?" she called back.

There was a long pause before the sheepish answer came: "Both?"

Despite her worried attitude, Tessa looked like she was trying not to laugh.

"There's a first-aid kit in the restroom, Jimmy. Do you need help?"

There was another worrying crash that made her wince, followed by, "No, ma'am, I've got it."

Melody looked at Tessa for commiseration. Her friend's eyes danced with humor.

"Think about it, Tess," Melody whispered. "If I go into hiding just because some guy my brother once arrested is running around loose, I'm going to have to leave Jimmy in charge of the store. I mean, *think* about that for a minute."

"What happened to that other employee you used to have? I can't remember her name—Mary?"

"Martha. She was great. I wish I hadn't had to let her go; she used to work here back when it was still Autumn Pages, you know, before I bought the store. She's helped me so much over the last few months. But she's having another baby—that makes four for them, if you can even imagine it. Her husband has a good job with the Forest Service, and she's planning to stay home for a couple of years."

"I'm definitely staying home," Tessa declared, spreading her fingers over the round curve of her pregnant belly swelling out her oversized T-shirt. The T-shirt had a picture of a basket of kittens with PURR-FECT! in script letters above it. "I know I'm lucky that I can. But I'm so *tired* all the time. I don't know how Gaby manages to run her café with two little kids."

"She has her mom to help her," Melody pointed out. She didn't begrudge her friends having happy marriages and babies, but there were times when it drew uncomfortable attention to her own single state. *Like I even have time for a boyfriend, busy as I am with the store.*

"True. And I guess she's not even doing that right now."

Melody paused in the middle of reshelving a Dan Brown thriller. "They're not closing the café, are they?"

"Not permanently, but for the next couple of weeks," Tessa said. "With Nils Sorenson running around loose— Ghost, I guess, is his street name; it's what Ben and Derek call him, anyway—they don't want to take any chances."

"That's a big step." Melody knew how much Gaby loved her little bakery and sandwich shop. It had been her dream, in the same way the bookstore was Melody's.

"*Yes,*" Tessa said emphatically. "You see how seriously they're taking this? Melody, this guy almost killed Derek and Gaby two years ago. And you've *met* Derek; you know what he's like."

Melody nodded. Gaby's mate was a big, well-muscled, dangerous-looking guy who could've graced the cover of one of the Navy SEAL romances over in her Romance section. If Gaby hadn't been head over heels for him, she might have been a little bit nervous around him. It made it easier that she usually saw him behind the counter in the Brown Bear Café down the street, wearing an apron and handing Gaby trays of doughnuts.

"Are they going out of town?" Melody asked.

"They're talked about it, but right now they feel like they'd be safer here," Tessa said. "We're all staying at Derek and Gaby's farmhouse with at least one of the guys there at all times. Gaby didn't want to disrupt the kids' lives any more than they have to."

9

"You and Ben are there too?" They really *were* taking this seriously.

"Yes, us too. Come on, Mel, at least move into the farmhouse with us for a little while. There's plenty of room. And that little place you're renting is *not* secure. I know that you think you're safe because you can turn into—that thing you turn into—"

"Can you please talk about this a little quieter?" Melody glanced around nervously to make sure no customers were near enough to hear any of this. Jimmy had gone off to the bathroom, and the only other person in sight was a little old lady browsing in the Garden section.

Still, now that she'd finally managed to realize her dream of owning her own bookstore, and was working hard to get it off the ground, the last thing she wanted was to have her customers find out her bookstore might be the target of an escaped convict out for revenge.

Let alone any of them finding out that the soft-spoken bookstore owner, with her dowdy gray cardigans and glasses, was actually a dragon. Yeah, that'd be good for business, all right. Tessa was human, and even though she was mated to a shifter, Melody didn't think her friend understood the fear of discovery that all shifters lived with.

Tessa at least had the decency to lower her voice, but she still looked worried. "Melody, it doesn't matter what you turn into if someone whacks you over the head or shoots you."

"Miss?" the little old lady said with a smile, puttering up to her. "I'm ready to check out now, and that nice young man isn't at the register."

"I'll ring you up right away," Melody told her. As the woman puttered off with her basket of books, Melody patted Tessa's arm. "It's sweet of you to worry. But I don't need your worry. I'm fine."

Tessa grabbed her hand and squeezed it. "I just think about you all alone in that apartment. Ben worries about you too. At least come down to the farmhouse for a few days. Melody, *please.*"

Melody thought of her apartment, her new lair, cozily filled with books, arranged just how she liked them. Every dragon yearned for a safe place to curl up and spread out its hoard. She'd only just gotten used to having moved her entire book hoard from the city to her new, smaller apartment in Autumn Grove. This place was finally starting to feel like home. And now, the idea of moving somewhere new, even if it was just across town, filled her with dread.

But Tessa was looking at her with wide, worried eyes. "Even if you think you don't need our help, if anything happens, you can help protect *us*, right?" Tessa said hopefully. "With your dragon. We *need* you."

It was clear that her friend wasn't going to take no for an answer. Melody's resistance finally crumbled. She patted Tessa's hand and forced a smile. "Yes, okay, I'll pack a bag tonight, and only my most important books." She could fit a little of her hoard into a suitcase. Maybe another box or two of books in the trunk of her car. There were so many she hadn't read yet! It was hard to find new books to read when there were so many old favorites to reread ...

"Miss?" the old lady called from the register.

"I'm coming! Do you need a lift home?" she asked Tessa. She might not be worried for herself, but an escaped convict posed a danger for her human friends.

Tessa shook her head. "Gaby is picking me up." A car horn honked outside. "Oh, there she is." She hung onto Melody's hand. "We'll see you tonight at the farmhouse, okay?"

"Okay," Melody sighed, giving in.

Giving in as she always did, she thought as she went to the front of the store to ring up the customer's books. She caught a glimpse of herself reflected in the glass of the countertop: a drab little woman dressed in gray, her black hair pinned up, the glasses perched on her nose giving her a schoolteacher air.

She'd always been steamrolled by stronger personalities around her. Growing up in the shadow of her father, a powerful dragon clan leader, it was easier to just tell him whatever he wanted to hear than to try to fight back. And she loved Tessa like a sister, but her best friend was so stubborn that Melody usually ended up going along with Tessa whenever they argued.

Like this situation, for example. After a long day at the bookstore, she just wanted to go home, make herself a cup of tea, and open a book. She didn't *want* to go to Gaby and Derek's farmhouse, which she knew would be full of cats and clutter and kids.

Sometimes she felt like she had spent her life being an accessory to other people's lives, letting their opinions overrule her own. She wished she could have someone who would *listen* to her, who respected her desire for quiet and privacy and order.

Dad says that most dragons don't have mates, which means there probably isn't someone perfect out there for me. Her parents weren't mated, and it showed; two strong-willed dragons, they couldn't be in the same room without arguing. She hadn't exactly grown up with good relationship role models.

Maybe she should try dating, even though it had largely been a disaster in the past. There might not be a Mr. Perfect out there, but perhaps there was someone she could have fun with.

Single man wanted. Must love books ...

Yeah, right. In this town? Three quarters of her customers were female, and most of the others were buying books for their wives or girlfriends or moms. Most of the men in

Autumn Grove were big, physical guys who liked working with their hands, not exactly reading types. And the good ones were all married anyway. Her chances of stumbling across an unmarried male bookworm looking for a girlfriend were about as good as her chances of suddenly meeting the fated mate she was pretty sure she didn't have.

Heck, even her one employee didn't seem to like books all that much. He certainly couldn't put them on the right shelves to save his life.

"You look so sad, dear," the customer told her as Melody bagged up her books. "Do you know what my mother used to tell me when I was sad?"

"What's that?" Melody asked, trying to smile.

"She used to tell me there's a silver lining to every cloud, and a rainbow follows every storm. It'll get better, dear. Just wait."

Melody held the door for her, and then turned to look around the bookstore. Afternoon sunshine slanted through the windows, painting the books' spines in soft shades of gold. She drew a deep breath, inhaling the smell of old paper and bookbinding glue, and in her chest she could feel her tense, stressed-out dragon begin to uncoil and relax.

All her life, she'd yearned to have her own used bookstore, and now Hidden Treasure Used Books was no longer a fantasy but a wonderful reality. Even if the building was old and things were always breaking, even if she was already having trouble finding customers and realizing why Autumn Pages had gone out of business ... No, enough with the negative thoughts.

No matter what happened in the next few days, she reassured herself, everything would be all right. Her friends would be fine. She'd have her book hoard and her store.

So why did her life seem empty to her now? Why did it seem as if there was a part of her that truly did yearn for the clutter and cheerful chaos of Derek and Gaby's farmhouse, rather than wanting to retreat to her quiet apartment full of books?

I'm lonely. But that's okay. I have friends who love me, and I just need to keep busy with the store until this whole escaped-convict thing blows over. And then she could go back to her life, and nothing would have changed. Nothing at all.

GUNNAR

The ride from the prison was quiet and tense. Gunnar sat next to the cop, Keegan, looking out the window as warehouses and factories gave way to suburban houses and then woods and small towns.

"We're going out in the country?" he ventured. He was wearing the clothes he'd been wearing when they booked him, a slightly shabby brown suit. Three years since he'd last worn it, the seams strained at his shoulders and it was too loose in the waist. He'd bulked up and lost weight around the middle since he'd last been a free man.

On his lap he held a small bundle of items in a bag. Wallet, some cash, the keys to an apartment and car he no longer possessed, a phone with an expired plan, a few books and magazines he'd had in his cell ... it was literally all he had in the world now. He wondered what had happened to the stuff in his apartment after he was arrested. Probably the landlord had thrown it out.

"It's a little town called Autumn Grove," Keegan said, glancing at him. "Ever heard of it?"

Gunnar shook his head.

"Good," Keegan said, and looked back at the road.

Keegan had put on a pair of sunglasses, and without being able to see his eyes, Gunnar found his expressions hard to read. He suspected Keegan was some sort of shifter, but wasn't sure exactly what made him think that. It was something about the way he moved, the casual animalistic grace, and the way he made Gunnar's bear nervous. Some kind of big cat, Gunnar thought, or maybe even another bear.

Even without being able to read Keegan very well, the distrust came through loud and clear. Gunnar really didn't blame him, especially if he'd known Nils.

Are we going to fight Nils? his bear rumbled. It was enjoying the freedom, but seemed unsure about that. *Nils is our brother. We shouldn't fight him.*

We're not going to fight him unless we have to, Gunnar told his bear. *But if he tries to hurt anyone, we won't have a choice.*

His bear was distracted from the argument by the woods outside the car. *Are we going there? We can shift there!*

For a moment, it was all Gunnar could do to contain the animal inside him. Surrounded by humans, he hadn't been able to shift for the last three years at the prison. The urge to get back in touch with that side of himself was a desperate ache like a hole in his chest.

"You okay?" Keegan said. "Hungry?"

Gunnar's stomach growled. He'd missed lunch at the prison—not that there was much to miss—and they'd been driving for hours. "Little bit," he said.

"We'll eat when we get where we're going." Keegan hesitated; Gunnar could tell he was on the verge of saying something. What he finally said, though, wasn't what Gunnar had expected. "What were you in prison for?"

Gunnar eyed him, suspecting a trap. "You know that already, right? I'm sure you've read my file."

"I know what your file says. I want to know what *you* say."

Gunnar hesitated for a few long moments. Finally he said, "I wasn't a good kid. I used to get into trouble. It'd be easy to blame it on Nils, because he was my big brother, my role model. But I really don't have anyone except myself to blame. I dropped out of school, got in trouble, got caught doing things like stealing cars. Spent some time in juvie." He took a deep breath. He didn't like talking about this part of his life. But it had happened; he couldn't change it. "I finally hit a point where I could see that if I didn't go straight, I was going to get one strike too many and spend the rest of my life in prison. So I got a job, kept my nose clean, and tried to turn things around. Then ... then Nils showed up three years ago."

It still hurt to talk about it. His brother had come back into his life after having vanished for years, used him as an alibi and stashed stolen goods at his apartment, and then skipped town when things got too hot and left Gunnar to the cops. Whatever they'd once shared as brothers was gone ... or so he'd been telling himself for three long years in prison.

"I told the cops and the judge that the stolen stuff wasn't mine. But I had a record, and I couldn't afford a better lawyer than the public defender, who had a ton of cases and wasn't really that invested in mine. I mean, look at me." Gunnar gestured to himself with one big hand. "I don't look innocent. Apparently the judge didn't think so either. I got ten years."

"That's a lot of time when they don't really have you on anything other than holding stolen property. Because of your record?"

Gunnar shrugged with a lightness he didn't feel. He could lie. But he had a feeling Keegan had checked up on him thoroughly enough to know all of this already. This was a test, all right. It was a test to see how much of the truth he was going to tell.

Even though the truth could make Keegan turn this car around and take him right back to prison.

17

"They offered to cut me a deal. Let me go, or at least give me probation, if I turned state's evidence against Nils and helped them catch him."

"You didn't take the deal," Keegan said quietly. "So they threw the book at you."

Gunnar nodded. There was no surprise in Keegan's voice. He'd known all of that already. It really had been a test.

"I know why you're asking me all of this," Gunnar said quietly. "I wouldn't betray my brother three years ago. So what you really want to know is, why did I agree to help you this time? You want to know if I'm just in it for an opportunity to escape."

"The thought did cross my mind," Keegan said, his voice bland.

"Look, if there's one thing I had plenty of time to do in prison, it was think," Gunnar said. "I spent a lot of my life telling myself that blood was more important than anything else. Nils and I ... we're all we have in the world. Our parents died when we were kids. We don't have any other close family. I used to feel like, if I lost my brother, I'd lost everything."

He drew a slow breath to calm himself and his restless bear, and wished he had sunglasses like Keegan's to hide his eyes. Instead he looked out the window.

"But I guess what I figured out in prison is that Nils hasn't felt that way about me for a long time," he said. "And even if he still did ... he's done a lot of bad things. *Really* bad things. He's killed people. I started feeling like prison was exactly where I deserved to be, for letting him get away with it for so long. I took your deal because I want to make things right."

"Even if it means helping put Nils away for good."

Gunnar nodded.

"Hmm," Keegan said, and didn't say anything else.

He turned off the road and drove through a small downtown. It was late afternoon now, and Gunnar looked out at the little brick buildings with the golden sunlight slanting between them. For some reason his eyes were drawn to a sign reading HIDDEN TREASURES USED BOOKS, with the colorful display of books in the window. He wanted all the knowledge inside those books. He wanted to be the kind of person who was worthy of it.

He turned his head to watch a group of children playing in a small park on the street corner. Two of them were little blond boys who reminded him of himself and Nils at that age. Would his life have turned out better if he'd grown up in a place like this? Or would he just have found some other way to screw it up?

"Something interesting out there?" Keegan asked sharply, and Gunnar shook his head, trying to shake off the echoes of the past at the same time. "Good. The place where I'm taking you ... well, let's just say, there's some trust involved in me taking you here. Mostly it's because I want you where I can keep an eye on you. I thought about putting you up in a motel, but you could skip out easily from there, or get a message out to your brother. This way, someone's going to be watching you every minute. Got it?"

They left town, turning onto a small road that went back into the trees. "You're taking me home with you?" Gunnar asked, disbelieving.

"Actually, I'm taking you to a friend of mine's place. His name is Derek, and he's the one your brother is gunning for. He's a mean fighting machine, and he turns into a big damn alpha grizzly. Don't think you can take him in a fight—and yes, I know you're a polar bear shifter, like Nils."

We're going to fight another bear? his bear asked, perking up.

No! Gunnar thought at it, horrified. *Don't you dare!* The last thing he needed was to get sent back to prison because his bear, after so long being cooped up inside him, lost control at the first dominant bear it came into contact with.

"His family's there," Keegan said. "Mate and kids. My mate too, and make no mistake, if you harm one hair on *any* of their heads, you won't be able to run far enough or fast enough. Derek and I will hunt you down and tear you apart."

"I won't." Gunnar tried to infuse the words with every ounce of honest sincerity he possessed. "I swear to you, I'd rather die than let harm come to anyone else because of my brother."

"Lucky for you, my animal lets me know when people are lying." Keegan's voice was close to a growl. "That's the only reason why you've made it this far."

He turned off the road onto a gravel driveway that stopped at a gate made of heavy bars of metal. "Stay in the car," Keegan said, still with the growl in his voice. He started to get out, then stopped and held out a hand, palm up. "I saw a phone in the things the guard gave you. Give it to me. You'll get it back when you leave."

"It doesn't even have a service plan," Gunnar pointed out, but he handed it over as requested. Keegan pocketed it and left the driver's door open while he went to the gate.

Are we going to fight him? Gunnar's bear wanted to know. *I'd really like to fight him.*

No, we aren't going to fight him. We aren't going to fight anyone. Settle down and be quiet.

He leaned forward and watched Keegan open the gate. It wasn't just a matter of unlocking it. Keegan punched a code into a key pad mounted on the steel pole beside the gate—Gunnar recognized it as an alarm system, and tried to stop the juvenile-delinquent part of himself from figuring out how hard it would be to turn off. There was also a wire wound around the top of the pole and gate that Keegan unhooked and left dangling while he swung it open.

As Keegan got back into the car, Gunnar said, "Don't normally see this kind of security on a farm."

"Yeah, well, most farms don't expect to be attacked by an escaped killer who turns into a giant polar bear, either." Keegan drove through the gate and left Gunnar in the car again while he went back to close the gate and re-arm the alarm pad.

This, at least, gave Gunnar some time to look around. Bathed in late-afternoon sunlight, the farm had a dreamy quality. It looked like something out of a movie, Gunnar thought, the sort of movie where little kids with braids and fluffy golden retrievers would be running through the grass in slow motion.

The main farmhouse was a big, rambling structure surrounded by a sweeping expanse of lawn. There was a wooden pole fence circling a barn and pasture. No slow-motion golden retrievers, but Gunnar saw a cat sunning itself on the top bar of the fence, and a small black-and-white pony browsing in the pasture. Some chickens pecked around in a wire-enclosed run beside the barn.

It was beautiful and peaceful and very much not a place for a guy who'd just spent three years in prison.

Gunnar's throat tightened. All through the drive, he'd thought the hardest part of all of this was going to be dealing with his brother. But this was the first time he'd felt panicked. For an instant he just wanted to tell Keegan to turn around and drive him back to prison.

I can't do this. I can't sit around with this nice farm family and pretend I'm like them. I'm not like them. I may not have done what I was sent to prison for, but I was a teenage car thief. I'm not a good person. I don't belong here—

"Hey!" Keegan said, leaning into the driver's side. "You can get out of the car now. Unless you want to sit out here all evening, but if you do that, then *I* have to do that, and I'll miss out on Gaby's amazing home cooking."

Gunnar got himself under control and made sure his bear was firmly under control. "Coming," he said stiffly, and got out.

They walked past several other vehicles parked outside the house: a sleek black Mustang, a minivan, and a little hatchback with some dings and rust spots. Interesting bunch of cars, Gunnar thought. He wondered if it was an equally interesting mix of people inside the house.

As they climbed the steps to the old-fashioned wooden porch, the door burst open and a woman ran out. She was visibly pregnant and had light brown skin and bouncing dark-brown curls, and that was all Gunnar had a chance to see before she flung her arms around Keegan and planted an enthusiastic kiss on him.

Keegan kissed her back just as enthusiastically. Gunnar couldn't believe the change in him; he'd thought the guy had a stick up his butt a mile long, but for this woman, Keegan's stiff cop face dropped away, revealing a grinning lovesick fool underneath.

The kiss broke and the woman's knees visibly wobbled. Keegan steadied her with an arm around her pregnancy-swollen waist. "Wow," she murmured, and then whacked him in the shoulder with the back of her hand. "You're late—" She stopped, noticing Gunnar on the lower step. "Oh ... hi. This is ...?" She looked blankly at Keegan.

"Ghost's brother Gunnar," Keegan said. "I need to talk to Derek before we go in the house. Is he inside?"

"Yeah, he's with Gaby in the kitchen." She turned to Gunnar with no sign of fear, and held out a hand. "Hi, I'm Tessa."

Gunnar started to reach for her hand, but Keegan put an arm around her, pulling her back.

"Hey!" Tessa protested.

"Don't go getting friendly with him," Keegan said. "He's here because we need him and because I want him where I can see him. It's strictly business."

"That's still no reason not to be nice." Tessa freed herself gently but firmly, and turned back to Gunnar. "I'm sorry that my husband has no manners. Anyway, I'm Tessa, and—"

The door slammed open for the second time, this time hard enough to bounce off the wall with a tremendous crash. "What the hell, Keegan?" a deep voice roared.

For a moment it was all Gunnar could do to keep his bear under control. The big guy who'd just stomped out onto the porch was pure dominant shifter grizzly from his bristling buzz cut to his size 13 boots. Massive shoulders strained against his T-shirt, and tats sleeved his arms. The bear inside him was so close to the surface that he had to be right on the verge of a shift; Gunnar could see it in his eyes.

"Calm down, Derek," Keegan snapped, holding out a hand to stop him. Derek was taller than Keegan by several inches and had probably fifty pounds of muscle on him. Still, Keegan didn't seem afraid of him in the slightest.

"We agreed we'd get him out of prison," Derek snarled. "Nobody said anything about bringing him to *my home*, where *my family* is—"

"And mine!" Keegan snarled back. "You think you're the only one with something at stake here? I brought him here not only because I believe he genuinely wants to help, but also because at the farm, we can watch him; he can't go running off to find a phone and call his brother—"

"So get him a guard! Or an ankle monitor! Don't turn my *home* into—"

"Are you reacting this way to *him*," Keegan shot back, "or is it because he looks like his brother? Stop letting your animal think for you. Calm down and consider this like a rational human being and not—"

"My animal *is* me, and I am him," Derek growled. "And right now he's telling me to rip this guy's throat out before he can take one step toward my mate and cubs."

Gunnar breathed deeply, keeping hold of his bear as it tried to lunge out of him. Getting into a fight wouldn't do him a damn bit of good. Even if he won, he would still have lost, because they would never trust him again.

"Derek, he's right," Tessa said. "You need to calm down."

"Stay out of this, hon," Keegan told her. "Go in the house."

"*Excuse* me? What kind of alpha-male nonsense is this?"

Keegan didn't take his eyes off Derek. "You're human, Tessa; you haven't seen how shifters can get when their animals are riled up. I don't want you to get hurt."

"You do remember I faced down a dragon, right?" Tessa said, her voice icy.

"You're right," Keegan said, the corner of his mouth twitching. "In that case, do me a favor and, for their sake, keep Gaby and the kids inside until things calm down out here."

"Now that, I'll do." She edged around Derek carefully and vanished into the house.

"Look what he's done to us already." Derek's voice was a low rumble. "We need to show a united front against Ghost, and now we're falling apart. Bringing him here was a mistake, Ben."

"I'm starting to think you're right," Keegan began, then turned his head at the sound of tires crunching in the driveway. "Are we expecting anyone else?" He reached across to his shoulder holster.

"The girls said your sister might show up."

"Damn it," Keegan muttered. His hand still hovered near his gun. "That's just what we need."

Gunnar's bear didn't want him to take his eyes off Derek, in case of a sneak attack, but he turned along with the rest of them to look down the driveway. From here, all he could see was a shadowy figure at the gate, undoing the security system as Keegan had done.

The gate swung open and the new arrival drove through in a little silver Miata convertible. The top was down, and Gunnar got a good look at her as she maneuvered into a parking place in the row of cars.

He would never forget that first look.

She was bathed in the golden light of late afternoon, turning her pale skin to honey and lending a golden sheen to her hair like a crown of liquid night. As she got out of her car, he took in the gray cardigan and the glasses, and his initial thought was that she looked like the world's sexiest librarian. Her buttoned-up sweater did little to conceal the luscious curves underneath. He wanted to unwrap her like a gift. He wanted to feel those ample breasts pressed against him, cup his hands under the bountiful curve of her ass ...

His newly arrived librarian goddess looked up at the scene on the porch. Behind her glasses, she frowned in puzzlement, and then her eyes met Gunnar's and—

It was like lightning striking. There was something charged and heated in her eyes. He was aware of the rustle of wings, the slow ripple of silver scales. And behind all that, a shocking conviction that Gunnar and his bear both knew, deep down to their shared core.

This woman was his mate.

MELODY

This man was her mate.

Melody stared up at the huge blond stranger on the porch, while her dragon writhed in excitement inside her.

Bathed in the glow of the sun setting behind the trees in the pasture, he was golden from head to foot, with short blond hair like a crown of gold, and the planes of his face lit as if by firelight.

Of course he's a fit mate for us, her dragon enthused. *He's made of gold!*

You don't even hoard gold, you silly creature, Melody scolded fondly. *For us, he should be made of paper and bookbinding glue.*

But her gaze stroked his face as if by proxy for her fingers, from the high forehead (intelligent, because of course any mate of hers must be), down the broad angles of his cheekbones, across a slightly crooked nose that helped keep his face from being too symmetrical and pretty, to full lips that she could so easily imagine caressing her own—

She gasped at the surge of want coursing through her and dropped her gaze away from his lips, but that was worse, because then her eyes went down to the tuft of golden hair peeking out of the collar of his shirt (no, not there!), down to the large capable hands that she could picture gripping her waist as he bent her over the hood of her car—

She wrenched her face away from him, her cheeks flaming. She couldn't believe the thoughts she was having, with the entire family there! It felt as if they should be able to look inside her head and see the lust that felt as if it would consume her.

Her family ...

Now that she'd managed to tear her gaze away from the golden vision of Adonis on the porch steps, she became aware, belatedly, that something was going on. Something ... intense. That was Derek, Gaby's mate, in front of the door, and he was all but bristling. Even without being able to feel his bear's agitation the way she could have recognized an angry dragon, she was aware of his fury; it had weight and force, as if protective menace rolled off him in waves, making her want to step back.

Her brother stood between her golden Adonis and Derek, and he was in what she recognized as Full Cop Mode, one hand even resting on his gun. Not to use it against Derek, surely?

"What's going on here?" she asked. Her voice cracked on the first word but she managed to gain control over the rest of the sentence.

"Long story," Ben said. "Sis, why don't you go in the house and check on how Gaby's doing with dinner?"

Her Adonis threw Ben a sharp look at the word "sis," and Melody's eyes narrowed. Ben seemed to be deliberately making a point of their relationship, which made her wonder why. For her mate's sake, to warn him away?

But of course he didn't know the Adonis on the porch steps was her mate. Her Adonis was now looking at her with clear blue eyes, as blue as summer skies and tropical oceans —eyes that were strangely tormented.

"This was a mistake," he said suddenly. His voice was a deep rumble that seemed to vibrate up from the center of his chest, and Melody's dragon thrilled to it. "This was a mistake, Keegan. Take me back."

Back? Melody thought. *Back where?*

Ben laid a hand on his arm. "Calm down, Gunnar. You've come this far—" and the rest of his sentence was lost, to Melody's ears anyway, in her dragon's delight at learning their Adonis's name. Gunnar! What a perfect name, so strong and masculine. It rolled off the tongue, with musical overtones that reminded her of his voice, deep bass notes to complement the lighter harmonics of Melody's name—

"That's right, take him back to prison where he belongs." Derek's snapped words cut through Melody's distraction, overriding her dragon's rapture.

Wait. Prison?

"No one's going to prison," Ben said in exasperation. "No one is going anywhere. Derek, between you and me and— our third, we can easily control him if anything goes wrong." He glanced at Melody, delicately declining to mention her dragon; even among their fellow shifters, dragons were reclusive and secretive.

But what was all this about *controlling* Gunnar, as if he were something dangerous? And ... *prison?* She tried to catch his gaze, but he stared at his feet and refused to look at her.

She was taking in more details now, though. The cheap, ill-fitting brown suit—she hadn't even noticed it before, too distracted by the shoulders inside the suit. The glimpse of blue tattoo ink on the back of one of his hands—that wasn't a *jail tattoo*, surely?

It was not possible that she'd found her mate only to have him turn out to be some sort of felon. Not a fellow bookworm who would delight in the same quiet scholarly pursuits that Melody loved, but some sort of common ... criminal?

But there was no other conclusion she could come to, particularly with the way Derek was looking at Gunnar as if he might lose control and attack them all at any moment, the way Ben was standing near Gunnar with "cop mode" on, not just as if he wanted to protect Gunnar from Derek, but as if to protect the rest of them from Gunnar ...

Melody stared in appalled disbelief.

There is absolutely nothing wrong with our mate, her dragon insisted, though its earlier delight had given way to uncertainty. *Our mate is perfect for us. Look at that jaw! Those arms! We just need to give him a cha—*

Oh, shut up, Melody told her dragon.

GUNNAR

s a younger man, Gunnar had dreamed about the day he'd meet his mate. He didn't know what she would look like, what color her hair or skin would be, what her voice would sound like, what kinds of things would delight her. He knew only that she would be perfect, and in her eyes he would see all the best parts of himself reflected.

Never had he imagined that she would stare at him in appalled horror. And who could blame her? What did he have to offer this lovely, curvy librarian-goddess with her soft voice and soft hands? He'd just spent the last three years with the roughest dregs of society. Hell, even before that, he had a rough past and the criminal record to prove it. Even if she could somehow, by some miracle, look past all of that, his brother—and Gunnar's own moral failing in refusing to condemn Nils while there was still time—was the entire reason why all of them were in danger. Of all the times when he could have met his mate as a younger man, it had to be now, when he was too broken and ugly to have anything to offer her anymore.

The more she learned of him, the more she'd loathe him. What could he even say in his own defense? The best thing he could do for her was stay as far away from her as possible.

His misery was so deep that he barely cared that the standoff had broken and Derek now seemed willing to let him into the house, though with visible (and understandable) reluctance. Right now he wished he could be anywhere other than here.

Three years in prison had, at least, given him skill at hiding his real feelings. He was able to muster a veneer of friendliness as he was introduced to Derek's mate Gaby (small and pretty, with a round face framed in dark waves of hair), Gaby's mother Luisa, and Gaby and Derek's children Sandy and Jimena. Gaby was a consummate hostess, greeting him with such friendliness that no one would have guessed she'd just witnessed her husband threatening to throw him out by bodily force. Gaby's mother even came up, stretched on tiptoe to pinch his cheek, and declared that he was too pale and needed to eat more.

At the family table, he found himself sandwiched between Derek and Keegan—not by accident, he knew, and he had no illusions that it was a place of honor. His mate, whose name by now he'd managed to figure out was Melody, was down at the other end of the table next to Tessa, physically as far away from him as she could get. That was probably no coincidence either, he thought, and tried to force himself not to consider it a hopeful sign that she kept darting glances at him down the table from behind the lenses of her glasses. Instead he made an effort to muster up some appetite for the delicious-looking bowl of chili and fresh-cut homemade bread that had been passed down the table to him.

The family were talking about regular family things with almost aggressive levels of normalcy, chatting with 7-year-old Sandy about the swimming class he was taking over the summer, asking Tessa about an online class she was apparently taking. Gaby and her mother took turns feeding little Jimena in her high chair.

He heard someone say "... bookstore?" to Melody, and his bear perked its ears up.

"Oh, it's doing as well as can be expected," Melody said. She had a soft voice, and throughout the family conversation she'd been doing little more than mumbling into her chili; he had to strain to hear her. "It's early days yet, of course. I'm having to pick up a clientele. I want to do more book sales online, because there's a big market for that. Autumn Pages didn't even have a Facebook page, let alone a website, and I think if I'm able to do something like that, it'll help my business a lot."

Her voice picked up as she warmed to the topic, becoming more engaged and excited. Her excitement was infectious, lifting both Gunnar and his bear out of their misery. And, he thought, of *course* she owned a bookstore. Because she was perfect for the man he yearned to be, and wasn't.

"You have a bookstore?" he asked before he could stop himself. "Is it that one downtown? I saw it when we drove in."

His words were followed by an awkward silence. Melody made a faint sound as if she'd started to say something, then looked down at her bowl of chili.

"Dessert," Gaby said briskly. She got up from the table. "Who wants dessert? I had to clear out the baked goods from the shop, so there's an entire smorgasbord to choose from. How about I just bring a big tray to the table?"

"I'll help," Melody said, jumping up.

After they'd left, Keegan turned to Gunnar and said quietly, "Hey, just for the sake of family harmony, I think it'd be better if you kept your distance from my sister and our mates. You don't need to know where Melody works, because you aren't going to be showing up where she works. Understand?"

Gunnar nodded wordlessly.

He'd finally found his mate and he couldn't even talk to her. And they were *right*. He was nothing but a danger to her.

Anyway, it was clear that she didn't want to talk to him, either.

After a round of amazing pastries (Gunnar managed to find his appetite here; tempting baked goods weren't exactly in large supply in prison) the family swung into helping with cleanup, with everyone pitching in. "I'll wash dishes," Gunnar told Gaby, finally seeing a chance to be helpful and pouncing on it.

"That would be wonderful, thank you. You can wash and I'll dry."

"I'll dry," Derek declared, looming abruptly. "You've been on your feet cooking all afternoon. Go put your feet up and enjoy the company in the living room."

"I would do that in an instant if I thought you weren't trying to separate me from our guest." Gaby stood on tiptoe to kiss him. "Why don't *you* go put your feet up, and I'll dry dishes and make our guest feel at home."

Derek made a low sound in his throat, one step removed from a growl. He gave Gunnar a long, threatening look before skulking off into the living room.

And suddenly, surprisingly, they were alone in the kitchen. It was the first time Gunnar hadn't had a crowd of people around him since he'd gotten to the farm. Voices and laughter came in from the living room, and he could occasionally glimpse Derek or Ben finding a reason to wander past the kitchen door and look in with an ominous expression, but after three years of prison it was almost like having privacy.

Gaby turned on the tap, held a finger under it, nodded at the temperature and moved on to put the dishes into the sink as it filled with suds. Gunnar hovered, not quite sure whether he ought to say something, or move in and help. She stepped aside after the sink was full, picking up a dish towel, and nodded to him.

He took her place at the sink with relief. Give him something to do with his hands, any day. He tried to force himself not to think about his mate and imagine what she was doing in the living room. No matter how hard he told himself he had to stay away from her, he was still drawn to her, the way true north tugged at a magnet.

"Ben said you never did anything violent," Gaby said quietly. "He said you ran with a bad crowd when you were young, but you never hurt anyone, and you only went to prison because you wanted to help your brother. Is that true?"

"I haven't exactly lived a good life. I won't lie about that." He hesitated. "But ... I guess it's true."

"Good." Her pretty face relaxed into a smile, and he found himself smiling back. Her friendliness was infectious. She took a bowl from him and began to dry it. "You do look ... very like your brother, you know. It's hard for Derek, especially."

"I know." He glanced sideways at her. "What did my brother do to you and Derek?"

"Are you sure you want to hear this?"

"I'd rather know." He was glad Melody wasn't here, listening in, though in all likelihood she already knew the story; the whole family probably did.

"It was two years ago." Gaby gave a small sigh as she neatly and efficiently stacked the clean, dry bowls. "I was working at a coffee shop in the city, before I had the café. I witnessed an armed robbery involving your brother and he came after me. I ... er ... I saw him shift. That's how I found out about shifters."

Gunnar swallowed and focused on washing every tine of a fork. He could picture it easily. Nils was absolutely terrifying as a bear. He was huge, the biggest bear shifter Gunnar had ever seen. If that had been her first introduction to shifters, it was amazing she was willing to be around them at all.

"Did he hurt you at all?" Asking the question felt like pressing on a bruise. He didn't want to hear the answers, but he was driven to know.

"No. Derek protected me."

There was warmth in her voice, and when Gunnar sneaked a peek at her, he was amazed to see her looking at him with warmth in her eyes, too. She laid a small, gentle hand on his arm.

"You're not your brother, Gunnar. Derek looks at you and only sees Nils. Sometimes I do, too. But even though Nils almost killed us, I can't hate him, not really. Not like Derek does. It was because of him that I met Derek, and I wouldn't change that for the world. Sometimes the darkest clouds have the brightest, most silver linings."

Silver linings. He thought of Melody, imagining it was her hand on his arm instead of Gaby's. If just being in the same room with her made him feel the way it did, what might touching her feel like?

He heard a sudden cascade of laughter from the living room, and knew instantly that it was hers. He'd never heard her laugh before, but he knew its quiet music like he knew the sound of his own breath.

"Come on," Gaby said briskly, taking the fork from his hand and not seeming to notice his distraction. "Let's finish this up and I'll make up a bedroom for you and give you a quick tour."

~

The house had seemed large to Gunnar even from the outside, but compared to the parade of low-rent apartments he'd spent his life in (let alone a jail cell), it was an absolute palace. There were four bedrooms: a master bedroom and the baby's room upstairs, Sandy's room downstairs, and another, very small bedroom behind the kitchen that was normally used for storage, that Gaby told Derek she was going to make up for him.

"I'd like to give you more room," she said as Gunnar helped her move the boxes that were stacked on the bare mattress. "But I think you probably wouldn't want the bedroom right next to mine and Derek's, and Tessa and Ben have already taken the bigger downstairs bedroom. We moved Sandy up to stay in his sister's room, but Melody can have that one, and both kids can sleep in our room for a few days."

"What about your mother?" Gunnar asked, stacking boxes where she showed him. The room was cramped and dusty, but it still beat the hell out of Cell Block D. "I thought she lived with you."

"She does. She's got her own cottage on the property." Gaby laughed as she snapped a sheet across the mattress. "I love my mother dearly, but living in the same house with her is a disaster. I mean, can you imagine sharing a house with your mother for your entire life?"

"I never had a chance to know."

He instantly wished he hadn't said anything when she turned large, sad eyes on him. "Oh, Gunnar. I'm sorry."

"It was a long time ago." He paused, distracted. The bedroom's single small window was open to let in the breeze, and in the blue dusk outside, he saw Melody and Tessa walking across the grass. There was no mistaking

Melody. Just as he'd know her laugh, he would also know her step, the way she moved, the way her hair fell over her shoulder ...

His bear strained toward her. He ruthlessly suppressed it. Did her animal also yearn toward him, that silver-scaled serpent he'd so briefly glimpsed inside her?

"Oh, they're going to get the cats," Gaby said, seeing where he was looking. "Do you like cats?"

Gunnar struggled to tear his mind away from Melody. "Uh ... I like 'em okay, I guess? I haven't really been around cats much."

"But you're not allergic or anything."

He shook his head.

"Good," Gaby said. "Tessa and Ben have four, and since they're going to be staying here a few days, they brought the cats along. The problem is, we already have two, so right now their cats are shut up in the barn. We're going to try putting Ben and Tessa's cats in one of the bedrooms and see how that goes. Our cats are indoor-outdoor farm cats, and theirs are mostly inside cats, so if the weather's nice ours can spend most of their time outside, which will help reduce the risk of cat fights."

"How many animals do you have?" Gunnar asked. He hadn't realized when he first got here that it was a real farm, with a barn and everything.

"Two cats, about a dozen chickens, and the pony. You can meet her in the morning. Her name is Princess and she's a sweetheart. We got her for Sandy when a neighbor was looking to rehome her," she rambled on, pulling the sheets tight before laying a quilt across the bed. "I always wanted a pony when I was a little girl, but we lived in a tiny apartment, so it wasn't going to happen even if we could have afforded it."

Gunnar nodded along, but his gaze had drifted to the

window again. Melody and Tessa were coming back from the barn, each with a cat carrier.

"There!" Gaby declared, and he looked back quickly to see her looking over the room with her hands on her hips. "Sorry it's still so cluttered, but at least there's room in here to sleep. We can move the rest of this mess out to the barn tomorrow."

"It looks great," Gunnar said honestly. "I mean, last night I had a jail cell to sleep in. This is worlds better."

He wished he could take back the words when an awkward silence descended.

The front door slammed as Tessa and Melody came in. With some effort, Gunnar managed not to run into the living room like a lovesick puppy. Instead he waited while Gaby plumped up the pillows, and then followed her back out to the living room.

Melody was there.

She was sitting on the couch, feet tucked under her and sleek dark head bowed over a book. She looked like a picture in a magazine. He could already imagine what her skin would feel like under his hands, its infinite softness. He ached to go to her, to touch her.

The sound of the baby crying came from upstairs, and Gaby turned with a soft "Oh!" and hurried up the stairs, leaving them both alone.

Now was his chance.

Melody seemed to be lost in her book. Gunnar wet his lips. Stupid ... he felt like he was back in middle school, trying to work up the nerve to say hi to the girl he had a crush on. Someone could walk in on them at any moment. He wasn't sure what Keegan would do if he caught Gunnar talking to his sister.

I could tell them I'm her mate ...

Yeah, and get sent straight back to prison, do not pass go, do not collect $200.

While this inner battle was taking place, he'd been slowly approaching, step by step. All he needed to do was say hello. She was his mate; everything would fall into place from there, wouldn't it?

"Melody—" he began.

"Gyaaahhh!" She jumped and the book went sailing several feet away and landed upside down in a sprawl of pages.

"Sorry!" Gunnar said, stepping back quickly.

"Homigosh. It's just. You. Wow." She pressed one hand to her chest and pushed up her glasses where they'd slipped down her nose. "You're *very* quiet. I had no idea you were there, and then you were just there—*looming*—"

"Didn't mean to sneak up on you. I, uh. I'm really sorry."

"It's okay. I get so wrapped up in my reading sometimes that I lose track of time." She smiled at him, and his stomach flipped over. She was so gracious, and so kind.

And now she was leaning down to pick up the book that she'd dropped because of him. "No, let me," he said quickly, and knelt to pick it up and hand it back to her.

"Thanks," she said, taking it back. Their fingers brushed against each other, warmth and softness slipping across his callused fingertips before retreating again.

And now he was kneeling by her knees, an improvement over the earlier situation in that he was closer to her, but he couldn't think how to gracefully get off the floor without looking like an idiot and also looming again. Plus, where did he go from there? Sit on the couch? Try to have a conversation while standing over her?

Why was this so *hard*?

Also, it didn't help that he was acutely aware he needed

only to move a few inches and he could have laid his hand on her leg ... or buried his head in her lap ...

Instead, they stayed that way for a tense moment, with Gunnar kneeling awkwardly by her legs, before Melody cleared her throat and patted the couch next to her. "Would you like to sit?"

"Yes," he said gratefully. He scrambled from floor to couch, trying not to go through an intermediate "looming" stage.

"I know this must be as strange for you as it is for me," she said, and smiled at him. That smile was like sunshine; it warmed and soothed him. "How about we get to know each other a little bit?"

"Okay," he agreed. What he really wanted to do was lean across the space between them, cup her face in his hands, and find out if her cheeks were as soft as they looked, and if her lips tasted as good as the rest of her smelled. But talking was good. Talking was great, actually, if it kept him here on this couch, listening to the melodious sound of her voice. She was aptly named; she sounded like a melody ... except she wasn't saying anything right now. Damn. Was he supposed to start?

"Oh ... kay," Melody said, into the silence. She smiled again, looking a little more nervous this time. "Let's start with a fun question. What's your favorite book?"

"My favorite book?" His mind went completely blank. People had favorite books? "I, uh ... I'm not sure?"

"Oh, I know," she said, warming up. "It's hard to pick, isn't it? I mean, I certainly couldn't pick just one. My desert island book list is more of a suitcase. Or possibly a U-Haul truck. What's the last book you read, then? For me it was, well—" She picked up the book in her lap and turned it over with a smile. "*Jane Eyre*. I know, I've read it so many times already, but that's the great thing about books, isn't it? They're like old friends you keep coming back to. And look at me, babbling." She took a deep breath and mimed zipping her lips.

"You don't have to stop," he said quickly. "I like hearing you talk ... about books." And it was true. She could be reading the menu and he would enjoy it. "Is that one your favorite?" he asked, pointing to the book in her lap.

"*Jane Eyre*? Well, I suppose it's *one* of my favorites. It's an old comfort read from childhood. Of course, I have a lot of those ... but you must too, right? Tell me about one of yours."

"Um." His mind went blank again. Put on the spot, he couldn't think of a single book. He liked to read, at least he really *wanted* to like to read; it was just ... books didn't like *him*. Reading was always such a struggle. All he could think of now were a few books he'd had to read for school, a very long time ago, that had been boring and not his kind of thing at all, but he didn't think she'd like to hear about those. What if she wanted to talk about one of them? He couldn't even remember their names.

"Gunnar ...?" His name even sounded lovely on her tongue, with that melodious lilt to her voice. "Gunnar, you do ... *read*, don't you?"

"I, uh ... not much? I mean, I *can*," he said quickly, just in case she thought he was completely illiterate. "It's just, you know. Kind of not my thing?" he finished with a certain amount of desperation, because she was looking at him with actual despair.

"You don't read?"

"I can if I have to!" he hurried to say.

This didn't seem to help. She looked devastated. "You haven't read *Jane Eyre*, then?" she asked in a small voice, holding it up.

"Never even heard of it."

41

"Oh." The book dropped into her lap along with her hands. "Do you ... want to?" she offered tremulously.

He'd caught a glimpse of the pages when he picked it up to give it back to her. All that tiny type. It looked like a boring, eyestrain-inducing nightmare. "Maybe?" he said uncertainly.

Melody looked like she wanted to cry.

"So, uh ... what else do you like to do?" he asked as brightly as he could manage, knowing he'd upset his mate and still not quite sure why. "I like working out. And, uh— they showed movies in the prison on Thursdays—" Her despair took on shades of horror. *No mentioning prison! Abort! Abort!* "What's your favorite movie?" he asked hastily.

"I, um ..." She twisted her hands in her lap. "I don't really ... watch movies, Gunnar. I'd rather have a nice evening with a good book."

"You never do *anything* except read?" he asked in bafflement.

"What else is there worth doing?"

They stared at each other in mutual incomprehension.

Given how the getting-to-know-you was going, Gunnar was almost glad (almost, though not quite) when they were interrupted by a slamming door and a sudden yell from upstairs. It sounded like Tessa's voice. "No! Don't let them— look out below! Gaby! Help!"

Gunnar and Melody both looked toward the stairs in blank confusion. There was a pattering of ... feet? Then a swarm of cats appeared on the stairs and hurtled off in all directions. Tessa popped into view an instant later at the top of the stairs, her hair sticking up in all directions. She grabbed onto the railing at the top of the stairs to stabilize her very pregnant body and looked down the stairs into the living room, where not a single cat was visible. For a minute, no one said anything.

"I don't suppose," Tessa said at last, huffing for breath, "that either of you two saw where they went."

Melody had her hands over her mouth and was making tiny squeaky sounds as she tried not to laugh. Gunnar hesitantly raised a hand to point at the kitchen. "I think one of them went in there?"

A baby began wailing from upstairs. Gaby's voice could be heard making hushing noises. "Oh no," Tessa sighed. "I'm sorry!" she said over her shoulder, and began to descend the stairs carefully.

Melody took her hand away from her mouth, cleared her throat, and pointed to her feet. "I think there's one under the couch," she said, her voice steady, with only the dancing of her eyes behind the lenses of her glasses to give away her amusement. "Do you want me to see if I can get it out?"

"Yes, please," Tessa said with relief. "Bending and twisting aren't so great for me right now. Or anything that needs me to be light and quick on my feet. We had the cats all nicely shut in one of the upstairs bedrooms and then I tried to leave and ... well, you can see how that went."

Gunnar got off the couch and crouched down. Maybe he could help with this. He'd always liked animals. He could just glimpse the reflection of the cat's eyes under the couch.

"I can't reach," Melody reported, after stretching and trying to get an arm under the couch.

"I could pick up the couch, maybe?" Gunnar suggested.

Tessa had crept over to peek cautiously into the kitchen; now she turned around. "No, don't do that. They're completely freaked out from being shut up in the carriers, and I think all of Gaby's cats are out in the yard right now, so there shouldn't be any fights. I'll put out some food for them and see if I can coax them out that way."

"Oh, there's another one!" Melody whispered, pointing to an orange-colored cat that had just crept out from behind a bookcase near the door and was looking cautiously around the living room with its tail puffed up.

All three of the humans froze. Gunnar even tried to make his bear be quiet, though it wasn't like the cat could hear it.

"Hey there, baby," Tessa crooned, crouching down to bring herself closer to the cat's level. "How about you come to Mama and let's go back to the nice bedroom, huh?"

Just then a key rattled in the door, five feet away from the cat. The door started to open. Gunnar expected the cat to duck back behind the bookcase, but instead, sensing freedom, it made a dive for the widening crack between the door and frame.

As Keegan appeared in the doorway carrying an armload of groceries, there was a chorus of "Stop that cat!" and "Shut the door!" from Tessa and Melody.

Keegan looked down calmly and, swift but casual, moved a foot to intercept the cat's break for freedom. It was obvious that he'd had a lot of practice at this. He leaned down to scoop the cat up with his free hand and closed the door with his hip. Then he stood and looked at Gunnar and Melody crouching next to the couch and Tessa squatting in the kitchen doorway.

"Cats settling in okay?" he asked mildly.

"Oh yes," Tessa said, her voice serene. A spotted cat peeked around her legs and zipped away when she made a move to reach for it. "As you can see."

"I hope they haven't gotten my gun this time."

"No, not yet anyway." Tessa grabbed the doorframe, made a grunting sound, and settled back into a crouch. "By the way, dear, I think I'm stuck."

The corners of Keegan's mouth twitched as he suppressed a smile. He handed the cat to Melody, gave Gunnar a flat look that probably was meant to convey something along the lines of *Stay away from my sister,* and went to give his pregnant mate a hand up.

"So we get to spend the rest of the evening playing find the cat—ouch—and I woke up Gaby's baby," Tessa said dolefully as Keegan hauled her to her feet.

"It's fine," Gaby said, coming down the stairs with a sleepy-looking Jimena draped over her shoulder. "If she goes down for the night this early, she'll be up at 3 a.m. anyway."

As Gaby joined the group in the living room, Gunnar could see that any possibility of talking to his mate alone had slipped away utterly. In fact, his mate herself slipped away before he could stop her, quietly taking the cat off to put it in a bedroom. He gazed after her and wished he'd managed to find the right words. It didn't matter if they had all the time in the world if he couldn't do anything other than alienate her every time he talked to her.

This was going *great* so far. At least it couldn't get worse.

"Who's up for Pictionary?" Gaby asked brightly.

Okay. Maybe it could.

MELODY

She couldn't sleep.

It wasn't the bed, although given the crowding, she'd had to make do with a cot on the floor of the baby's room. Her twin bed back in her apartment was almost as small. No, this was a different problem, a problem with blue eyes and short, scruffy blond hair; a problem with cheekbones to die for and pecs that made her ache to run her hands over them.

And he wasn't her type at all. He wasn't even remotely her type.

He's our mate, her dragon told her, infuriatingly smug in its certainty. *He may not be what we thought we wanted, but he's what we need. That's how it works.*

But that's not how I work, she thought miserably, rolling over again and tucking her arm under the pillow.

She'd dreamed of meeting someone she could have long conversations with, about history and philosophy and her favorite plot twists in the latest bestseller. Instead she'd gotten someone who barely knew which end of a book to

BEAR IN A BOOKSHOP

start reading from, someone whose inner life was no more rich and exciting than his bear's.

That's unfair, her dragon told her snippily.

It *was* unfair ... but being mated to Gunnar meant spending the rest of her life with him. Every day. Every night. And even if the sex was good—who was she kidding; with a body like his, the sex was going to be *great*—she couldn't imagine what they'd spend all those evenings talking about. Was her life with a mate going to be exactly like her life before—quiet, lonely evenings spent reading by herself?

She sighed and gave up on sleep. Quietly, she dressed and cracked her door open. The hallway was dark and silent, the door to Derek and Gaby's bedroom shut. She stepped out into the hallway, gasped and stifled a curse as something soft and furry nearly tripped her.

A cat shot past her ankles into the room. Melody glanced back to see a tail vanishing into the warm nest of blankets she'd left behind.

"Don't let Tessa see you or you're going back into cat prison," she whispered.

Prison made her think of Gunnar. She grimaced. Everything made her think of Gunnar right now.

Carrying her shoes, she padded down the hallway and tiptoed down the stairs. She wasn't sure where she wanted to go; a half-formed idea had entered her head, a possibility for one way she might be able to get out of this unresolvable mess with Gunnar, but mostly she just wanted to get away for awhile. It was a dark night, with no moon: a good night for flying.

"Hey there," a quiet voice said out of the darkness in the living room, and she almost jumped out of her skin.

A moment later, her eyes adjusted enough to make out Gunnar sitting on the couch. As far as she could tell, he was just sitting there in the dark.

"What on Earth are you doing?" Melody whispered fiercely. She leaned over to put her shoes on and give herself something to do other than stare at him. "You nearly gave me a heart attack. Again."

"Sorry," he said quietly. "Uh ... sorry again, I guess. I didn't realize you didn't know I was there."

Her irritation slipped away in amusement, at herself more than him, and she laughed softly. "I should put a bell on you or something, so I'll always know where you are. You're so quiet. I don't think I've ever met anyone as big as you who can make himself as unobtrusive as you can."

It made her think of herself, actually, though she didn't want to say so. She wasn't big, of course. But she, too, had a way of hiding in a room while still being in plain sight.

Except for that one brief conversation on the couch, they hadn't had a chance for a single private moment during the entire rest of the evening. No opportunities to smooth over the awkwardness; no chance to find out what his big, capable hands felt like on her skin—

No! Stop that!

Gunnar got up off the couch. "It's something you learn," he said quietly. "When you've been—where I was."

"Prison?" she asked.

In the near-darkness, he was nothing but a shape, his blond hair backlit softly by the slight luminescence from the windows. She was acutely aware of him, though—aware of every inch of him. He was still a few feet away, but it seemed as if she could feel the heat of his body from here.

As if nothing separated them but the night. As if she already knew the taste of his skin, the feel of his body against hers—

"I can't pretend it wasn't what it was," he said softly. "That I'm not what I am."

"Neither can I," she said, but she took a step forward. He

did, too, as if they were drawn to each other by some magnetism greater than either of them.

It didn't have to matter, she thought. There were other things to do in life than talk about books. Things that needed no words at all ...

But when the dream ended and she woke from the heat of his hands on her skin, woke to find him lying beside her in bed ... what then? An empty life, trapped together, unsuited to each other—like her parents?

Except her parents had not been tied together by a mate bond, so they had been able to walk away.

He started to say something, and then stopped. She reached out a hand, not sure what she was doing or why, and her fingers brushed across his T-shirt-clad chest. She sucked in a breath. He stood still, and then his hand came up to close over hers, gently curling around her fingers.

She'd dreamed, awake or asleep, of what his fingers would feel like on hers. It was just as she'd imagined, and better than she'd hoped. His hands were big, strong, and capable, the fingers rough with calluses as they brushed lightly across the backs of her own.

She stepped forward before she knew what she was doing. Her arm was a livewire and current arced down it, drawing her to crash into him. He lowered his head, in the dark, and their lips found each other's as if meant for it.

His mouth was hot, hungry, wanting. His hand cupped her face, fingers curling into her unbound hair; his other hand still trapped hers against his chest, pressing her palm to his accelerating heartbeat. She gasped against his mouth and wrapped her other arm around his back, pulling him against her, as if they could be made not two bodies, but one.

What am I doing? The thought surfaced from her lust-drunk mind, and she caught her breath, breaking the kiss, and pushed him away.

He stepped back, startled and hurt; she knew it without seeing his face. "Melody?"

"I'm sorry," she gasped. She could still feel his lips on hers. She could taste him. She knew what he tasted like now; she could never forget it. "I'm sorry—I—this was a mistake."

"I'm your mate, Melody," he said. She hadn't realized her hand was still on his chest; she'd used the leverage to push him away, but only as far as the length of her arm. "We're mates. We're meant for each other."

Desire thrummed through her blood. If she gave in now, if she let herself fall against him one more time, she would never get away.

"I'm sorry," she said again, and wrenched her hand away from his chest. Blindly, tripping over furniture, she stumbled to the door and fumbled with the locks until she undid all of them and wrenched it open.

"Melody—" Gunnar began, and the distress in his voice cut her to the bone.

"Don't follow me!" she snapped, because she could hear his steps coming after her. She softened her voice: "Please. I need to be alone for a little while. Please?"

"It might not be safe out there."

He was so close. She dared not look back, not with her arousal still so powerful that it made her limbs shake, made her hardened nipples press against her sensible cotton bra.

"You know what I am." She tried to make her voice hard, but it came out shuddering. She need only turn around, give in to what her body so desperately wanted—*No!* "Just as I know what you are. You saw my animal when you looked in my eyes. You know, better than anyone, that I need fear nothing when I walk in the forest at night."

But the words, which had always been true, were a hollow lie now. She feared nothing except her own emotions. She feared nothing except her animal's desire to bond her to a man in a union that could bring nothing but pain for both of them.

Her steps were swift, all but running, around the corner of the house and through the meadow grass to the barn.

Gunnar didn't follow, respecting her wishes—whether she wanted him to or not. Mingled relief and disappointment rose in her throat, choking her like unshed tears.

In the stillness of the night, she stood with her hand resting against the rough boards of the barn wall. Her breathing calmed; her racing heart slowed. Her knees no longer trembled.

She still wanted him like a fire inside her.

She also knew that once she had him, there was no going back from that.

Melody shook her head as if to shake off her own thoughts. There might be, just possibly, someone who could help her. Help *them*, because Gunnar was just as trapped by this unsuitable bonding as she was. It wasn't anyone she would ever have dreamed of talking to about her romantic woes before—but in this particular case, that person might be able to help her when no one else could.

She took off her glasses and tucked them into a pocket of her cardigan, having learned the hard way that while her clothes and anything in the pockets shifted when she did, her glasses and other accessories did not. The night was now an indistinct patchwork of light and dark blurs. She took a few steps away from the barn to give herself room, and shifted.

The blurry world shrank, but didn't get any clearer. She had often considered the possibility of having glasses custom-made in a dragon size, but the idea of how ridiculous it would look, let alone trying to explain to an optometrist why she needed her prescription in bicycle-tire-sized lenses, had always stopped her. Besides, her dragon's sharp sense of smell made up for their mutual lack of vision.

Oh, good, her dragon crooned, spreading great leathery wings. *If you're done being stupid about our mate, can we fly now?*

We can fly now, yes.

Hunting? the dragon wanted to know.

Not right now. Maybe later. Tonight we're going to see Father.

Oh, that's a long flight. I like that. This will be fun.

Her wings beat downward. It was hard to launch from the ground, much better to jump from a height, but after a few strong beats she lifted off, tucking her legs under her. Relying on the moonless darkness to hide her, she winged her way across the mountains, heading for her father's lair.

Flying across this rough country was faster than driving, with no need to follow the winding roads and highways, but it was still a long flight. Normally she would have welcomed the solitude and the opportunity for mental peace, but tonight her mind was in turmoil. She forced herself to focus on the rush of wind across her wings, the fuzzy haze of the stars above, giving herself over to her dragon's pleasure in simple, physical things. Soon enough, she glided down over the blurry lights of her father's mansion, perched on a clifftop overlooking a secluded valley.

She had worried that everyone would be asleep, but light spilled out onto the lawn. Her father often kept late hours. She landed on the grass and shifted, folding her wings about herself, and restored her glasses to their usual place on her nose. Although it was nice not to have to shift back naked, like non-mythic shifters had to, she felt severely under-dressed in her gray cardigan as she mounted the wide marble steps to the front door.

For a long time she had tried to be the daughter her father wanted. She had dressed like a haughty daughter of wealth when she was in his house, even though she felt like a child dressing up in someone else's clothes. And she'd left her glasses at home, even though she was half blind without them and contacts hurt her eyes, because he didn't like seeing her wearing them; he considered it shameful for one of their kind to advertise their weakness in such a fashion.

But these days she had retreated into a sort of pride in the dowdy, librarianish way of dressing that she preferred. She almost enjoyed her father's scathing looks when she came to dinner wearing jeans and a sweater, with her hair in a bun. It wasn't like she was ever going to be the tall, glamorous daughter he'd wanted, so why play the part anymore?

The door opened just as she reached to knock, and her father's manservant Maddox blocked the light, a massive slab of muscle crammed into a suit that always seemed slightly too small, somehow, even though it fit him perfectly. Expensive tailoring couldn't hide the enormous shoulders or the graceful, pantherlike way he moved.

"Your father's in his study," he rumbled, and glided out of the way. "He's expecting you."

"Of course he is," she murmured. It didn't surprise her that she'd been detected on approach. She knew that her father's security system was second to none. It wouldn't even surprise her to learn that some of his technology was military grade.

Maddox didn't bother escorting her; he knew that she knew the way. Her footsteps echoed down long hallways, and ornately decorated doors opened silently at a touch of her hand. Her father's mansion was like a museum, full of the gold and jewels and expensive artwork that he liked to hoard.

She vastly preferred her dusty, cozy apartment full of books.

The door to her father's study was closed. She tapped lightly and waited for his acknowledging "Come in" before entering.

She was privately glad that she hadn't found him in his

home office, a vast and austere room with tall windows looking down on the valley. His study was a more intimate space, full of dark wood paneling and old-world charm. A fire crackled in the fireplace (genuine; no gas-grill fakery for Darius Keegan) and the lamps, while electric, simulated the warm glow of old-fashioned lamplight. Her fingers ached to touch the spines of the leatherbound books lining the walls. Darius, with a glass of brandy in his hand, sat in a large leather chair in front of the fire.

"Father—" Melody began, and then stopped. She hadn't expected him to have a guest, so it had taken her a moment to notice the second chair was occupied.

The other man rose quickly, and bowed to take her hand and bring it to his lips. "Miss Keegan."

"Heikon Corcoran," she murmured. She was not over-joyed to see him, though as the heads of other dragon clans went, the lord of the Corcoran clan seemed to be a reason-able sort. It was just difficult to forget that they'd been on opposite sides when she'd met him and the rest of his clan, even though their dispute with her own clan had been resolved through Tessa's intervention.

"I can leave," Heikon said, making another brief bow with courtly old-world grace. He was much older than her father; she'd grown up thinking of Darius as unimaginably old, but Hiekon was one of the truly old dragons, born hundreds of years ago. He was old enough that he genuinely looked old, his hair gone mostly to gray and his face lined, unlike the ageless severity of Darius and most of the other adult dragons she'd met.

"No," Melody said. It occurred to her, given the reason why she'd come, that the wisdom of accumulated centuries might be exactly what she needed. If her father didn't know the answer, she would have had to seek out Heikon later anyway. "I can say what I need to say in front of both of you."

"Drink?" her father asked, pressing a glass into her hand before she had a chance to say yes or not. "It's good to see you, daughter." He reached out fastidiously to flick something off her shoulder. "You appear to have a cat hair on your ... whatever you call that garment you're wearing."

Melody glanced down self-consciously at her shapeless cardigan, then looked more critically at her father's dark velvet jacket. "As do you, Father," she said with a slight smile, and reached out to brush off a handful of orange and white hairs.

"That little pest," Darius remarked in a conversational tone. "I've told it to stop shedding, but will it listen?"

Melody rolled her eyes. She knew her father doted on the kitten Tessa had given him, now grown into a young cat. In fact, there he was, the orange and white tomcat with the undignified name of Toblerone (Tessa had named him; Darius had never bothered to change it). The cat was stretched out on a red velvet pillow in front of the fireplace, a pillow that Melody strongly suspected had been put there for cat-comfort purposes. She could see no other use for it.

But chiseling at the cracks in her father's emotional armor wasn't why she'd come. While she was contemplating her brandy and the cat, Darius had dragged another chair to the little grouping in front of the fireplace, and reluctantly, she sat.

"So tell me of my daughter-in-law and grandbaby," Darius said, smiling with a warmer expression than she was used to seeing on his face. "How is Tessa?"

Nothing about Ben, she couldn't help noticing. Her brother and father had mended fences, more or less, but it still wasn't a close relationship. She knew that Tessa hoped the birth of their child would change that, but Melody privately suspected some wounds were too old and deep to ever truly heal.

"She's fine. Just tired all the time." He hadn't asked about Nils, she noticed, which almost certainly meant Ben and Tessa hadn't told him and therefore didn't want him involved. Having an alpha dragon on their side wasn't a bad idea, but considering what Darius could be like, she hardly blamed them for wanting him to stay out of it. She decided not to break their confidence, for now.

"I recall Esmerelda was the same when she was pregnant with you." Darius smiled in recollection and swirled the brandy in his glass. "So what brings you by?" His voice was casual, as if she'd simply stopped in at a house down the street to bring over a casserole.

"I have a question." She wrapped her hands around her brandy glass and tried not to think of Gunnar's strong arms, the startling softness of his lips on hers ...

After tonight, if she got what she'd come for, it wouldn't matter.

"You know, maybe I *should* leave," Heikon said, leaning forward in his chair.

"One grows used to awkward questions when one has children," Darius said over the rim of his brandy glass. He looked amused by the rival clanlord's discomfort. "Particularly daughters."

Irritation helped embolden her. "Oh, please, as if I *ever* brought you my birds-and-bees questions. No, this is ... well, not entirely unrelated, I guess." The thought had now occurred to her that she was about to drop the news on her father that his daughter had found her mate, and it wasn't going to be good news. May as well just rip off the Band-Aid rather than dragging it out. "Dad, is there any way to dissolve a mate bond?"

There was a silence so profound that the crackling of the fire sounded suddenly very loud. Melody tried to distract herself by reaching down to stroke Toblerone's warm fur.

She couldn't help noticing that the cat pillow was located at just the perfect angle for Darius, in his chair, to lean down and pet its occupant.

"Why do you want to know?" Darius asked in a very level, very calm voice. Melody looked up and realized that, by leaning down to pet the cat, she'd put herself in a position where she was having to talk to him from the vicinity of his knees. She sat back up so quickly that she nearly spilled her brandy and leaned back in her chair as if she could press herself into the leather and escape the intent stares of the two dragon lords.

"I ... met my mate," she said in a small voice. "And I—it's not—he's not—I don't—"

I don't want to be mated to him, she tried to say, but her treacherous mouth stumbled over the words. Even without her dragon writhing unhappily in her chest, she knew that the words would be a lie. She couldn't stop thinking about his warm hands, his soft lips, and most particularly the hurt confusion in his voice when she'd turned away from him.

But we're terrible for each other, she thought desperately, trying to calm her dragon before her father sensed its agitation. *We have nothing in common. We would be miserable. I'm doing this* for *him. We should both be set free to find other people.*

Even to her inner ear, the words rang hollow.

Am I trying to convince my dragon, or myself?

"Don't tell me *you've* mate-bonded to a human too," her father said heavily. "Ben was bad enough, but I had much higher hopes for you."

Melody was caught off guard by the surge of protective anger rising in her chest, not just her dragon's but her own as well. *There is nothing wrong with our mate!* her dragon proclaimed.

"He's not a human," she said, hearing the anger in her own

voice; her father's eyebrows went up at that. "It's not about what kind of shifter he is."

"Well, that's ominous," Darius said. "What *is* he? A rabbit? A wombat? An *emu*?"

Heikon looked like he was struggling very hard to keep his impassive dragon-clanlord mask in place.

"He's a bear, if you must know," she burst out.

Darius relaxed slightly. "Oh, well, that's not so bad, as shifters of the regular animal kingdom go. There's a long tradition of intermarriage between the dragon clans and our fierce forest cousins. Does he come from a good family, at least?"

Now was the time when she should simply tell the truth and forever harden her father's heart against Gunnar, as she was trying to harden her own. *His family is the farthest thing from anyone's idea of "good." He's an ex-con, and oh by the way, remember that murderer who tried to kill Derek and Gaby not so long ago? That's his brother.*

Instead, she heard herself say, "I don't care about his family. I've never believed that someone's bloodline determines their worth. I just ... I just want to have a *choice*."

Darius smiled thinly. "A *choice*, daughter? You speak as if falling in love is like selecting your next book to read. If you're approaching it from that perspective, no wonder you're trying to flee."

"I'm not running away," Melody flared, as her dragon, affronted, spread its wings in her chest.

"Really? And yet," he said mildly over the rim of his glass, "you're here, asking me for paternal advice. I don't even remember the last time that happened."

"I would think you'd be supporting me in this," Melody snapped. "I've heard you say that you're glad you and my mother aren't mated."

"I said that? When did I say that?" Darius asked, his voice turning sharp.

"Er ..." It had been during one of her parents' fights, but she thought it best not to say so, if she wanted him to stay in a good mood. Both her parents, possessing even more than the usual amount of draconic pride, liked to preserve the polite fiction that their relationship had been calm, logical, and involved little emotion on either side, rather than being a stormy, tempestuous love affair that had broken up in the kind of fights that tended to flatten trees.

Anyway, the last she'd heard, her mother was "finding herself" on a luxurious round-the-world cruise and having an excellent time, so it wasn't like Mom was pining away for want of a mate herself.

The pause gave her time to gather her thoughts, but before she could speak, Heikon inserted himself into the conversation. "I might know a way."

Darius shot him an annoyed look. Inside Melody, her dragon cried, *No he doesn't! LA LA LA WE'RE NOT LISTENING—*

Hush, Melody ordered, to no effect, and tried to tune her creature out.

"Which old wives' tales were you thinking of, precisely?" Darius asked in a cutting tone.

"Concentrated essence of dragonsbane," Heikon said.

Darius stiffened in his chair. Melody was merely confused. "But that's a deadly poison," she said. The deadliest poison known to dragonkind, in fact.

"Not always. In less than lethal doses, it has other properties."

"None of which I wish to inflict upon my daughter." Darius's voice carried a low rumble of draconic anger; the sound of rustling, leathery wings could almost be heard.

"It's not your decision," Melody told him, and Darius gave

her a look of profound surprise. She wasn't in the habit of openly defying him; her own boldness startled her. "Go on," she added to Heikon.

The dragon lord steepled his fingers, elbows on his knees. "It is said, of dragonsbane, that it can be administered in a dose that leaves the human alive, but kills the dragon."

Melody sucked in her breath. "We don't want that!" she cried, hearing her dragon's distressed echo beneath her voice.

"I warn you, Heikon," Darius growled. "You are treading dangerously close to the limits of my hospitality."

"And of *my* patience." Once again Melody was shocked at the boldness she heard in her own voice. It was as if the mate bond had changed her on a deep level. She no longer felt like quite so much of a child in her father's house.

Heikon lifted his hands placatingly. "I meant no offense. Nor did I mean to suggest you should kill your beast; of course not. What I've heard, however, is that this property of dragonsbane can be used in extremely controlled doses to burn away the mate bond."

Melody's dragon was still so agitated in its horror that she had to struggle to control it. The mere mention of dragonsbane had sent it into a frenzy. Darius seemed no less horrified; his face was paler than usual, and she could feel his dragon's anger as he set his brandy glass aside, a heaviness in the air like the charged tension before a storm.

"Rumors and nonsense," he said sharply.

"I've heard of it being done," Heikon said, unruffled. "As an attack, of course, not something that one would choose to do to oneself. This was many years ago, in a rival clan of ours. The mate bond of the clan's alpha pair was severed with dragonsbane by one of their enemies, or so it's said."

"And they were unharmed?" Melody asked. "Their dragon or human side?"

"So far as I know. Of course, I'm not sure if 'unharmed' is precisely the word I would use." His dark eyes were intent on her. "Ending a mate bond is a psychic wound from which few can recover. It should not be done lightly."

"I assure you she is not planning to do it at all," Darius said. "Particularly not with something as dangerous as concentrated dragonsbane. Even touching it can be fatal."

Thank you, father; some sense at last, her dragon declared.

"Do either of you think you could let me speak for myself?" Melody said in profound exasperation.

"I apologize for any distress I've caused either of you," Heikon said. "I was only answering your question."

Darius glared at him before turning his fierce stare on Melody. "I hope you aren't considering this foolishness."

"Where would I even obtain dragonsbane? I haven't the first notion. It comforts me to know that there might be a way. That's all I really wanted, I think." She rose from her chair and set aside her untouched glass of brandy.

"We're not finished here," Darius began.

"Actually, I need to get on the road," Melody said. "Or ... on the wing. Whatever. I'd like to be back before they find out I was gone, or Ben and Tessa will have a fit; they'll probably think someone kidnapped me in the night."

She tried to force herself not to wonder about Gunnar's reaction. Would he worry? Would he think of her at all?

"I would hate to be the cause of unnecessary distress," Darius said dryly. "In that case, please convey my regards to my son's mate." He gave her a sharp look. "I trust you are not contemplating anything foolish."

"Do I have a habit of being foolish, Father?"

"No," Darius said, somewhat to her surprise, "but there's a first time for everything, and love makes people behave irrationally ... or so I hear."

"I'm not in love," she said, causing an anxious, desperate

stir of fluttering from the dragon nestled in her chest. She honestly had no idea if it was a lie or not, although the dragon clearly seemed to think so. She had to get out of here; she couldn't keep discussing this with her father. She was too afraid she'd give something away.

"Hmm. In any case, I suppose I will look forward to meeting your mate, daughter." This was said with a grimace of distaste that he didn't bother to hide. "Maddox will see you out."

"I know my way." She dipped her head to Heikon. "Good night."

She walked swiftly through the echoing halls of her father's mansion, and whether it was her dragon's doing or her own, her head was full of Gunnar: the sky blue of his eyes, the taste of his mouth, the way he looked when he smiled.

I just want to have a choice, she'd told her father.

She had spent her life giving in to what other people wanted for her. Now her body itself had betrayed her. Talking to her father had led to the surprising discovery that she wanted Gunnar enough that she was willing to fight for him. But ... was it really so wrong to want an escape hatch in case things went badly?

It's not running away. It's not. It's just ... wanting a choice.

She stopped when she realized where she was. Her wandering feet, as if they knew her mind better than she did, had taken her to the wing of the house where her father's office was.

His office. With his safe. Which she knew the combination to; from her years helping him with the family business, she knew all his passwords and access codes. And she was also familiar with the contents of the safe, including a few vials of something she was pretty sure was dragonsbane.

She let herself into the office. The huge, echoing space

was full of shadows, the only illumination coming from the tall windows that appeared as brighter stripes against the gloom. By memory and feel she found her way to the desk and switched on a lamp, then paused when she realized that the large oil painting of her mother that used to cover the safe had been replaced with a large oil painting of her father's cat.

Stay classy, Dad.

She lifted down the painting and set it against the wall. The same combination she'd memorized still worked. She shifted aside papers, boxes of jewels, and gold bars—not her father's entire hoard by any means, just a small and ever-changing part of it that he liked to keep near him—until her fingers closed on a small, rugged plastic case, looking very out of place among the other luxurious items.

Melody flipped it open. Three tiny vials nestled in the foam padding inside. There was a fourth space that was empty. She decided not to wonder what he'd used it for. Instead she took one of the vials very carefully, handling it with her fingertips. It looked so innocuous; tilting it, she saw there were only a few drops of clear liquid inside.

Concentrated essence of dragonsbane.

The idea of carrying it around in her pocket made her nervous. She wasn't sure if it could be absorbed through the skin, but she didn't want to take a chance, not just on her own behalf but also because of Ben, and because of Tessa's baby. How much dragon heritage did it take before a person was susceptible to dragonsbane? She wasn't going to use her loved ones as a test case. Instead she looked around for something to carry it in.

"Aha." In the top of one of the boxes of treasures, she caught sight of a locket on a golden chain. It was heart-shaped and crusted with diamonds, not something she'd dream of wearing normally, but for a hiding place for poison, it would do. The vial just fit inside, snugly enough that it was unlikely to roll around and break.

She fastened the gold chain around her neck and tucked the locket inside her sweater like the dirty secret that it was.

Insurance, she told herself, as her stomach knotted into a guilty ball. *That's all it is. A way out, for both of us, in case things don't work out.*

There was no guarantee she could get any later, she reminded herself as she put everything back, as close to how she'd found it as possible. If her dad realized that she knew about the poison in the safe, or even had thought of it as a possibility, he'd change the combination or hide it elsewhere.

I need this for you, Gunnar. For us.

So why did she feel so painfully, desperately ashamed?

GUNNAR

Breakfast at the farmhouse was an informal affair. The adults fed the kids, but otherwise, as far as Gunnar could tell, everyone got up when they wanted to, and fed themselves from a selection of cereal, eggs, and leftovers from the night before.

He'd awakened automatically at what would have been, for the last three years, prison wake-up call. Even before then, he'd drifted restlessly awake throughout the night. He had heard Melody come in, after having vanished for most of the night, shortly before the household began to stir. Lying in bed, listening to her soft, furtive steps on the stairs, he couldn't help wishing that those steps would turn his way, bringing her to his room to slip under the quilt beside him. She would be warm, yielding, her curves melting against him ...

He tried to force his mind to other things before he had to stumble half-dressed through an unfamiliar house with a hard-on and find a bathroom to masturbate in. Staining these nice sheets and the apparently hand-made quilt seemed like a poor way to repay Gaby for her friendliness.

But his dreams were full of Melody too, gray eyes like the sea and black hair that smelled like perfume and starlight. In his dreams, he was always searching for her, getting sad-eyed glances before she darted away. He knew that he should stay away—she'd be safer without him—but he couldn't seem to help following her, wherever she went.

Safer without us? his bear scoffed. *As if! We'll protect her from our brother or anything else that tries to hurt her.*

If only that was enough. The one thing he couldn't protect was her heart, and that was the thing, more than her physical wellbeing, that he risked by staying in her life.

When sleep finally deserted him completely, he got out of bed and poked guiltily through the contents of the shelves in the room. They contained a random mix of clutter that had overflowed from the rest of the house, canned goods and knickknacks, photo albums and books. A book on local history looked interesting. He sat on the bed, opened it to the first page—

—and quickly discovered that the text was, as usual, too dense and dry for him to read easily. Or, possibly, at all. He struggled onward for awhile, determined to beat it into submission through sheer effort, but when he found himself reading the same paragraph for the third time and understanding it no better than the first attempt, he gave up and skipped forward to the pictures and maps. Those were more fun.

When he heard sounds of the household stirring, he took the book with him to the kitchen. He tried to convince himself that the point wasn't to impress Melody that he'd been reading a difficult book, but ... well ... that kind of *was* the point, wasn't it?

Disappointingly, she wasn't anywhere in sight. All the other women were there, fussing over Gaby's baby. They saw him before he could slip off and everyone smiled at him, with a scattering of "hello" and "help yourself to whatever." Giving a nervous smile back, Gunnar got himself a cup of coffee and hovered awkwardly around the edges of the room for a little while before getting up the nerve to poke around until he found a box of Cheerios and a large bowl.

"When are you due again, dear?" Gaby's mother asked Tessa, patting Tessa's pregnant stomach.

"Only two more weeks, if they're on time." Tessa sighed. "From the size of me, not to mention all the kicking, I think little Whomever is as ready to come out as I am to have them out. I swear it feels like there must be a horse in there."

"It's not entirely out of the question, is it?" Gaby asked teasingly, looking up from wiping some of Jimena's breakfast off the high chair.

"A horse *shifter*, maybe. Better than an actual horse. I'm joking ... I hope." Tessa ruffled Jimena's dark curls, with little pink bows in them. "You've already carried one shifter baby. They don't ... you know ... *shift* in there, do they?"

"No, Derek says it takes awhile for the shifting to show up. Mina here hasn't shifted yet." She chucked Jimena's round, pink cheek. "We're not even sure if she's going to. She only gets the shifting from one side, after all."

Luisa turned around from the sink with a dish towel in one hand. "You should be so lucky if she doesn't. Running around after you was bad enough when you only had two legs. Imagine four! Might as well try to catch that little horse in the pasture out there—"

"Mama!"

It was all so warm and cozy and ... domestic. Even when Gunnar was a kid, his life had never been like this. There was nothing of the childhood he knew in this cheerful, sunny farm kitchen.

He took his bowl of cereal and cup of coffee, and went out the kitchen door. He was just planning to sit and eat on the back steps, but it turned out there was a little patio with a picnic table. He was sitting there, eating, and poking through the book again, when the door opened and Melody came out with a cup of coffee and a piece of toast.

"Hi," she said, smiling shyly. "May I join you?"

Her hair was down, like last night, framing her face in midnight-black waves. The urge to run his fingers through it was so powerful that he hastily picked up his coffee cup instead, to give himself something to do with his hands.

"Yeah, sure." He gestured at the bench-style seat across from his. "You don't need permission anyway. It's your house. I mean, I know it's not your house. But it's more like your house than my house."

While he mentally kicked himself for his complete inability to make casual conversation, Melody sat down and snuck a not-subtle peek at the spine of his book, tilting her head to the side and exposing a creamy length of neck, where a flash of gold was briefly visible. A necklace? It vanished as she straightened her head, hidden by the high collar of her sweater.

"That looks interesting," she said. "May I take a look?"

"Sure." He shoved the book at her and picked up his spoon to stop himself from leaving his hand on the book, hoping their fingers would brush.

It was stupid, the way he was behaving—like a kid with a crush. They'd kissed last night, hadn't they? He knew he had no right to ask for more, but ... he wanted more. So much more. But only if she was willing to give it, and he didn't know how to ask.

Melody opened the book to a random page. Upside down, he glimpsed solid blocks of text in paragraphs half a page long. Her eyebrows went up. "Oh," she said. "This is ..."

"Not the kind of thing you'd think I'd be into, right?" he

said, trying for a self-deprecating smile that he was afraid came out as more of a grimace.

"No, it's only ..." She took a deep breath and brought her hand up to her chest for a moment, as if to touch something there. Then she looked up and smiled at him. She wasn't wearing any makeup this morning; her lips were coral pink, a few shades darker than the tint of her cheeks. "Gunnar, I'm afraid we got off on the wrong foot yesterday, and a lot of that was my fault."

"There was lots of blame to go around," he offered. "Lots of wrong feet. A whole centipede of wrong feet."

Just as he was prepared to kick himself for saying something stupid, *again*, her laugh chimed; it was as musical as her voice. His heart skipped a beat. He'd done that. He'd made her laugh. He'd made her happy.

Do it again! his bear told him.

I can't exactly come up with witty lines on the fly, dumbass. I'm a felon who doesn't even have a high-school education, and she's—

Smart. Beautiful. Perfect.

Completely wrong for him.

"Where did you get this, anyway?" Melody asked, flipping the book closed with her finger in her place to read the cover.

"Off a shelf in the guest bedroom."

"I assumed you didn't ..." She hesitated.

"Read?"

"No ... no, I just—I didn't think this is the kind of thing you'd pick up for light pleasure reading."

"Well," he said, embarrassed, looking down at his coffee cup, "I didn't have anything else to do, and I was bored, so—"

This was still coming out all wrong. All he had to do, what anyone in his right mind would do, was slip in a smooth comment about how he read this kind of thing all the time. He could tell her he'd gotten tongue-tied earlier and given her the wrong impression—

—and then she'd ask him all kinds of questions about his favorite books, and he'd have to make stuff up and lie to her. Where they should be having a warm, casual conversation, instead it would be stilted and difficult.

What kind of relationship could they build on a bedrock of lies? He could pretend to be good at the things she was good at, but in the end she'd call his bluff and everything would come tumbling down.

Better to get the painful part out of the way in the beginning.

"See, the thing is," he said to his coffee cup, "it's not that I don't like to read. I do. I'm just not good at it."

"What do you mean?" Melody asked quietly.

He risked a quick glance up at her. She wasn't looking at him with condemnation or dislike. Her face was open, gray eyes curious and interested ... the way she might look at a book, he thought, a book she was trying to read, as if she had to puzzle through them the way he did.

"I don't have much education," he explained. "I was working on my GED in prison, but—books like that one ..." He gestured at the book in her hands. "The words just kind of all mix up together. There's too many of them, and too many big ones that are hard for me to figure out. I *do* like books. I'd like to learn to read better than I do. When I was driving into town—"

He stopped. It was harder to say than he'd expected. Like ripping a part of his soul open, exposing himself to ridicule or worse.

"Yes?" Melody prompted gently, leaning forward. She reached out hesitantly. Her fingertips danced along the end of his hand, making his breath catch.

"I saw your bookstore," he admitted. "I didn't know it was

yours, then. But I remember how I saw it and I ... I wished I could go in. It looked magic to me. Like a whole other world, so different from—" He stopped again, remembering how she'd reacted the last time he mentioned prison. But it had been his entire life for the last three years. It wasn't like he could just pretend that part of his life didn't exist.

"Like prison?" she asked softly, as if she'd read his mind.

"Yeah. I wanted to go into that world, but I felt like I didn't belong."

"I could show you," she said, very gently. Her fingers curled over the edge of his palm.

He turned his hand over, and she cautiously, uncertainly, placed her fingers in his rough, callused palm. Soft hands. Girl's hands. But not without calluses, he saw now, up close. She had a little callus on the middle finger of her right hand, from writing, and the tips of her fingers were faintly darkened, as if all that reading had left printer's ink permanently embedded in her fingertips.

"I really would like that," he said. "Maybe you could find me some books to read? Ones that aren't too hard, or too boring? Uh. I don't mean your books are boring. Just—"

He was cut off by the quick clasp of her hand on his. "Gunnar," she began, her voice warm.

Then she stopped, and they both looked up, at the sound of low voices and footsteps swishing through the dew-damp grass. Derek and Keegan were approaching from the direction of the barn. Derek had a shotgun slung casually over his shoulder; Keegan was wearing his shoulder holster and had leaves in his hair. Gunnar guessed they'd been checking the perimeter.

Melody's fingers slithered out of his and she sat back on her seat, reaching for her coffee cup. His hand felt bereft without her. His body yearned after her like a flower turning toward the sun.

"Funny how every time I turn around, seems like I find you with my sister," Keegan said to Gunnar. It was, Gunnar thought, not precisely hostile so much as wary, shading toward mild amusement.

"Funny how you think it's any of your business who I talk to," Melody said dryly. "Since I'm a grown woman. And that's not *all* I am, as you well know."

Gunnar was aware of the stirring of her dragon, the defensive rustling of its wings. He yearned to see it in all its glory, not these half-glimpses at the corner of his mind's eye.

"True," Keegan said with a half smile, not at all defensive. "I'm not here to break up the party, on purpose anyway, but we didn't get this guy out of prison just for coffee on the deck. Sorenson, I need to sit you down inside and start working on figuring out your brother's movements since he escaped. Old acquaintances, safehouses, anything you know that might help."

Gunnar nodded.

"After that—" Keegan began.

"After that," Melody said, "I was going to take him to the bookstore with me."

Gunnar had a feeling that he didn't look any less surprised than the other two men. Keegan gave both of them a long, searching look. "Are you sure that's a good idea?"

"I certainly don't plan to sit around the house all day," Melody said defensively. "He was interested in seeing the bookstore, so I figured I could take him to work with me."

"That's a terrible idea," Derek said flatly.

"Why?" Melody asked, looking from her brother to his friend, who was glowering at Gunnar. "Is it him you don't trust, or me? Or don't you think my dragon could keep him in line?"

Keegan cleared his throat loudly and pointedly. "We'll be inside. See you in a minute?" he asked Gunnar, who nodded.

After Derek and Keegan went into the house, Derek with a last glare over his shoulder, Gunnar said quietly, "Do you want to tell them?"

"About what?" Melody started to toy with the gold chain around her neck, then made a visible effort to stop, dropping her hand to her coffee cup.

"Us."

"You really think they'd react *better* if they knew you're my mate?"

"Well, at least that way they'd know why it was no use keeping us apart," Gunnar said—reasonably, he thought, but Melody looked down at her coffee cup.

"You should go help my brother," she said. "It's what you're here for, after all."

Things had been going so well, and now he felt like he'd ruined it again. At least this time it wasn't entirely on him; her family certainly wasn't helping. Like he could blame them, but still.

"You meant it, though?" he asked hopefully. "About taking me to the bookstore?"

Melody darted a quick look at him from under her lashes, behind the lenses of her glasses. "I meant it. As soon as you and my brother are done, we'll drive into town and you can help me open the bookstore." And her coral-pink lips curved in the faintest of smiles.

We. Just the two of them.

"I can't wait," he said, and he'd never meant anything so fervently in his life.

MELODY

Watching Gunnar in the bookstore was all she'd hoped for and more.

She'd had her doubts as she drove him there in her sporty little Miata (trying very hard not to think about his proximity, or her desire to reach over and put a hand on his leg). There were so many ways this could go wrong. She knew right down to her bones that he wouldn't hurt her, could *never* hurt her. But he might be bored. He might hate it. This might drive a deeper wedge between them, rather than bringing them together.

But as soon as she unlocked the door and they walked inside, she saw the look of wonder unfold across his face and knew that she'd made the right choice.

For the first half-hour or so, she let him roam the store while she rummaged around getting set up for the day. This was Jimmy's day off, so it was just the two of them. It looked like the weather was going to be nice, so she set out some tables of cheap paperbacks on the sidewalk in front of the store, got the café set up, and rearranged her window display before she went looking for Gunnar.

She found him in the kids' book section. He was sitting on the floor with a book open in his lap, and he looked entranced.

She didn't want to disturb him, though she tried to turn her head to see what book he was reading. She couldn't quite make out the title or cover. She turned her head more, twisting to the side—

Gunnar looked up, and jumped.

"Sorry!" Melody said, jerking back and knocking her elbow into a bookshelf.

Gunnar grinned. "Now I guess we're even. Maybe you need a bell, too."

"Maybe we both need to stop sneaking around," she admitted, and gestured to the book. "What are you reading? You looked like you were really into it."

His smile dropped away. "It's just a kid's book. Not like the kind of thing you read."

"I read all kinds of books." She crouched down to his level. "Just because it isn't full of hundred-dollar words doesn't mean it's not a good book. I haven't read every book in this store, but not for lack of trying."

This coaxed a small smile out of him. He turned the book over so she could see the cover: *The Story of Ferdinand*.

"Oh, this is a wonderful book," she said, smiling back. "I love this book. I gave a copy of it to Gaby for Sandy. Do you like it?"

"Yeah, I do." His hesitant smile turned into a full grin. "It's about a bull who doesn't want to fight like bulls are supposed to. I mean, he *can* fight, it's not like he can't, but he doesn't want to, even when the other bulls make fun of him for it. I like that he sticks to his guns and doesn't let them make him be what he doesn't want to be."

His gaze dropped back to the book, and Melody laid her hand on his arm. He was still wearing the poorly fitting brown suit over a gray T-shirt with a truck stop logo that he must have borrowed from Derek. He was turning the book over restlessly in his hands—big hands, deft hands, the fingers broad but sure.

Is that what you were like? she wondered. *A gentle child, who didn't want to fight? But everyone could only see what you were like on the outside, big and intimidating and scary, until they made you be what they said you always were.*

"I think it's a good message," she said gently. "I wish more people were like Ferdinand the bull. Do you want to keep it?"

Gunnar looked up at her sharply. "You don't have to give me books. You're trying to run a business here."

"I *want* to give you books," she said firmly. "And I think that's a good one to start with. It can be the heart of—" She stopped. *He's not a dragon. Normal people don't work like we do.* "It'll be a good book to build a library around," she said instead.

"I don't have a library." He gave a soft laugh. "First I'd need a house to put one in, anyway."

"One thing at a time. I can't help with the house, but I can help with the library. And ..." His arm was warm and strong under her fingers. She tightened her grip. "I owe you an apology, Gunnar. I've been a snob."

Gunnar frowned, his blue eyes puzzled. "No you haven't. You've been great."

"No, don't let me off the hook for it. I misjudged you, just based on the kinds of books you read. I'm sorry for judging you, and I ... I wanted to ask you something personal, if you don't mind. Away from the house, where the others can't hear."

"Sure." He didn't look defensive, just curious. "You can ask me anything."

"Have you ever been tested for dyslexia?"

He shook his head. "What's that?"

"You really haven't heard of it?" Melody asked, surprised.

"I guess it sounds a little familiar."

"But nobody ever gave you a test, or talked to you about it in school?"

He shook his head.

"Have you always had trouble reading?"

"It was hard to learn," he said. "Really hard. But I thought it was just because I was slow. That's what Nils said, anyway."

She hoped Nils did show up. She'd like to punch him in the face. "But the words get mixed up sometimes? People tell you that you're writing letters backwards, even though they look fine to you, or you just can't understand them when you look at them?"

Gunnar's face lit up. "Yes!" he said. "That's exactly what it's like!"

"I guess I shouldn't say for sure without having you tested for it, but that sounds like dyslexia to me. It's a learning disorder, a pretty common one. Lots of people have it. It doesn't have anything to do with intelligence, and it certainly doesn't mean you're slow. It just means that your brain processes letters and sounds differently than most people's."

"They get mixed up," he said cautiously, eyes on her face.

"Yes, kind of. I mean, if you think about it, reading is terribly complicated. You have to connect letters to sounds, and sounds to words, and words to their meanings, and then you have to put together all of *those* to build a word-picture in your head of what's happening in the book. And all of this is going on lightning-fast inside your brain whenever you read a page of text. It's no wonder that sometimes the wires get crossed."

Tentatively, he asked, "Do *you* have that problem?"

She wished, for a fleeting instant, that she could tell him they *did* have that in common, but it wasn't going to be quite that easy. "No, not me. But my mom does. It took her forever to learn how to read. We thought I might have trouble too, because it often runs in families, so she had me tested early. But it was never a problem for me; I took to reading like a duck to water."

"And ... what about your mom?"

"What about her?"

"Did she learn how?" Gunnar asked. The hope on his face was painful to see.

"Yes. I think she still struggles a little, but you'd never know. She has a Master's degree."

"So I *could* learn," he breathed. "I could get good at it."

"I'm sure you could. There are teaching methods now to help children with dyslexia. I can't believe no one ever talked to you about it."

He shook his head. "No, I guess I was always better at outdoors stuff, like sports, and everyone said I wasn't trying hard enough at the learning part of it. But I *did* try."

Melody spontaneously put her hands over his, suddenly and passionately furious at all those adults who had failed him, at his brother who had failed him, and made him think he was never good at something he *could* have been good at. Could still be good at. "It wasn't your fault. We can do something about this, Gunnar. We'll look up resources online, and I can call my mom and see what she says about it. And in the meantime, if you find books that look interesting and are easy for you to read, I don't care if they're children's books, okay? If you like them, then I'll help you find more. And don't even feel like you *have* to read if you don't want to, or force yourself if you don't enjoy it. It's okay for you to not want to. It's okay ..."

She ran down in a flood of babble, and stared down at their linked hands, curled on top of the book.

"Thank you," Gunnar said quietly.

Melody risked a glance up at him. He was looking at her

in a warm, soft, besotted way that she didn't think she deserved.

"You don't owe me thanks," she said. "I'm the one that should be thanking you, for ... for making me think about things in a different way." She took a deep breath, pushing herself past her hesitation. "There's something I want to show you, something no one else has seen. Would you like to see it?"

He nodded.

Melody scrambled to her feet. Still clutching *The Story of Ferdinand*, Gunnar followed her to the front of the store and then stopped when she flipped the sign on the door to CLOSED and threw the lock home.

"You know what I am," she said, turning around to look up into his eyes. "Just like I know what you are."

He nodded without speaking.

"What do you know about dragons?"

Gunnar shook his head. "I ... I didn't even know they were real 'til the first time I looked into your eyes. Which I guess sounds silly, coming from a bear shifter, but ..."

"No, it's not. We take care to hide ourselves, even from other shifters. And we're not quite like other shifters, not in all ways. We have special abilities. Special weaknesses." She had to stop herself from brushing her fingertips across the locket with its hidden, shameful secret. "And some of the old stories about us are true. We keep hoards."

Gunnar grinned, flashing his white teeth and making her knees wobble unexpectedly. "Are you telling me you manage a bookstore for a living when you have a stash of gold somewhere?"

"I do not hoard *gold*," she said primly. "What use have I for gold? Look around, and you'll see my hoard."

He looked around, and she could see the comprehension dawning on his face—on several levels.

"Oh," he said. "*Oh*. That's why ... when I said ..." He looked back at her, his blue eyes troubled. "Melody, when I said what I said about books, earlier—I had no idea. I knew you liked them, but I didn't know what they really meant to you."

"I know," she said gently.

She took his hand, heart beating fast as her fingers wrapped around his. The feeling reminded her of the first time she'd managed to bring herself to fly. During most of her childhood she'd been terrified of trying out her fledgling wings, despite her mother pushing her to take her first true flight. Finally she'd worked up the nerve to climb to the roof. She still remembered clinging up there on a dark night in midwinter—as dark as the city got, anyway—with her claws sunk into the shingles, scared out of her wits and yet excited. She remembered what it felt like to jump that first time, the weightless moment when her stomach lifted into her throat before her wings caught her and, for the first time in her life, she soared.

"Gunnar, I want to show you something no one else has ever seen. I want to show you the Heart of my hoard."

GUNNAR

fter Melody locked the door, she kept hold of
Gunnar's hand and led him through the aisles
between the bookcases, to a door marked
EMPLOYEES ONLY. She paused briefly before opening it.

Gunnar hardly even cared where they were going. She
could have led him anywhere. Her fingers were petal-soft
in his.

In his other hand, he carefully held the book she'd given
him, the one about the bull who was told to be cruel, but
decided to be kind instead, even though it went against what
everyone said his nature was supposed to be.

Maybe ex-cons could be that way too.

The EMPLOYEES ONLY door opened into a room that
combined the functions of storeroom and office. A small
desk with a single beat-up office chair and a folding table
were nearly invisible between, and beneath, stacks of cardboard boxes and heaps of books.

"I really need more help than just Jimmy," Melody sighed.
She let go of Gunnar's hand to move some boxes. Seeing that
she was trying to clear a space in the corner, Gunnar quickly

moved to help. They settled into a rhythm, Melody handing him boxes and Gunnar finding places to put them on the increasingly unsteady stacks.

"Who's Jimmy?" He managed to suppress his bear's growl of jealousy. She was his mate, and he was hers; it didn't matter who she talked to, or who she'd known before.

"My one and only employee, who unfortunately doesn't know a preface from an appendix when it comes to books. Ah."

Her box-clearing had revealed a small office safe. She knelt in front of it and dialed in a quick combination. With her hand on the safe door, she looked up at Gunnar, her eyes wide and vulnerable.

"Every dragon's hoard has a Heart," she told him. "It can be almost anything. My friend Tessa was once the Heart of a dragon's hoard, although she isn't anymore. And ..." She turned to the safe door and opened it. "This is mine."

She took out a small book and cradled it in her hands for a moment, running her fingertips reverently across the cover, before handing it up to Gunnar.

This was no treasured, leather-bound first edition. It was a thin, inexpensive-looking paperback, its cover scuffed, stained, and held together with tape. The pages were dog-eared and the book's spine was broken, so it wanted to fall open to the middle.

This was a book that had been *very* well loved by a small child. Gunnar held it with desperate care, afraid that it was going to disintegrate in his hands.

"*Where the Wild Things Are*," he read slowly aloud. With exquisite care, he opened it to a random page. The illustrations startled him, bold and cartoony and not at all what he thought Melody would like. No dense blocks of text here, just scattered words, easy to read.

Melody smiled shyly up at him. "It's about a little boy who

pretends to be a wolf—though when I was a child, of course, I thought he really turned into a wolf. I was so excited to find a book about a little child like me, a shifter child! And then he has adventures in a land full of monsters. In the end he has to go be a little boy again, just like I had to stop running around the house hissing at people, and shift back to a little girl and eat my supper and have my bedtime. But that magic place was still there, and I could go back to it any time I liked by opening that book. I read it over and over and over, until ..." She touched her chest, pressing her hand to the gray sweater. "Until it became part of my heart."

Part of her heart. Gunnar looked over at the Ferdinand book, which he'd placed on top of a pile of boxes while he helped Melody move stuff around. He hadn't really understood what she had been talking about yesterday, when she spoke of books being like old friends. Books couldn't be friends. They were just words on pages, words which had always opposed him at every turn.

But that was before he'd opened the Ferdinand book and started to read it, and he'd been startled to find out how much the bull, who was just a fictional character in a children's book, reminded him of himself. Sometimes a book could take the words that were in your heart—unspoken, unnoticed, maybe even hidden from you—and put them down onto a page.

And now he held Melody's heart in his hands, all fragile and torn up and patched with tape.

"You can read that, if you like." Melody's voice was soft and shy. "But ... uh ... I have newer copies out front, if you'd rather read one of those."

The pages that Gunnar had opened the book to, as well as being dog-eared and worn, also had crayon scribbles on them—red and orange loops, and a pencil scribble that looked something like a dog ... no, a dragon, playing with the rest of the monstrous creatures and breathing crayon fire. Drawn by Melody, twenty-five or thirty years ago. Carefully, trying not to dislodge the loosely glued pages, Gunnar turned to the first page, where he found what he had thought he might find: Melody's name, printed very carefully in crayon by the tiny hands of a child just learning to read.

Books were more than words; they were little pieces of personal history. Books were memories of reading, or being read to. He thought that from now on, whenever he read the Ferdinand book, he would always remember sitting on the colorful little patch of carpet in the children's section of Melody's bookstore, experiencing the book for the first time.

He wanted to treasure every page of this book, every little note or scribble that Melody had left there. He had to force himself to close it, and very carefully to hand it back to her. Gently and reverently, she put it back in the safe.

"I want to read it," he told her, and knelt beside her so she didn't have to look up at him. "I want to read it with you. And I'm going to. But not right now."

"What do you want to do now?" Her voice was hushed, her eyes dilated.

"This," he murmured, and leaned across the space between them to kiss her, for the first time by daylight.

She had offered him her heart; he could only offer his in return.

Her lips were soft and warm and responsive. She made a tiny gasp against his mouth and it went straight to his groin. He wanted her—*all* of her, not just the hot body that he knew she was hiding under those sexy librarian sweaters, but her sharp, compassionate mind and her deep emotions and her strong dragon's heart. The hurt parts of her, the scared parts of her, the parts were angry and the parts that weren't nice: he wanted those too. He loved—

He loved her. The realization hit as sudden as a slap.

84

"What is it?" She drew back and looked at him with puzzled gray eyes. "You stopped."

The sudden bolt of understanding had left him shaken. He loved every inch of her. Her eyes—he loved her eyes, in all their subtle shades of gray with hints of color (blue, green, soft hazel) when the light struck them just right. He loved the curve of her cheek, loved the dark strands of hair escaping from the severe bun she'd pulled it back into before leaving the house, loved her firm little chin and the way the corner of her full mouth quirked up slightly even when she wasn't smiling, as if at some private joke, giving her a Mona Lisa air of mystery—

"Gunnar? Is everything all right?"

"Thinking too much. That's all." He reached behind her head. "Okay if I take this down?"

She nodded, her head moving against his hand. She was still gazing into his eyes, her lips parted. He touched the hard knot of her bun and the clasp holding it in place, and undid it carefully. Her hair unwound from the bun in a dark water-fall, pouring down over her shoulders.

He yearned to see her clothed in nothing but that dark cascade. But he didn't want to rush it. He ran a thumb over her swollen lower lip, and her mouth opened responsively as he leaned in to kiss her again.

The first time had been cautious and tentative. This time she kissed him back like a wild woman, her mouth open and wanting, making gasping little moans. He let out a groan himself as he gathered her soft weight into his lap. She writhed against him, her hands all over him, skin touching skin as she slipped one hand into the gap between his T-shirt and the waistband of his pants.

Her gray cardigan was fastened up the front with a bunch of tiny little buttons. Gunnar undid them one by one. Beneath it, she wore a white blouse with little roses embroidered around the collar. Her nipples were erect, and he brushed his thumbs across them, drawing out more little moans, as he kissed and nibbled at her jaw and neck.

More tiny buttons to undo, and then her blouse parted to reveal her glorious breasts in a peach-colored cotton bra. The gold chain he'd glimpsed around her neck earlier was some kind of necklace with a locket dangling from it, nestled in the delicious valley between her breasts as if to call attention to it.

"If I'd known we were going to do this," she gasped against his shoulder as he reached around behind her to undo the clasp, "I'd have gone out and bought some sexy underwear—oh—"

The bra came free and he finally got a look at the naked bounty of her breasts. Her nipples were a darker shade of the same coral pink as her lips. Melody rose to her knees, and Gunnar lapped at her nipples while she raked her fingernails across his short hair and the back of his neck, panting.

He could smell her arousal. When he reached a hand between her legs, she jerked in reaction and pressed against him. He rubbed her through her jeans, feeling the hard nub of her arousal even with the fabric in the way. Too much fabric ...

"Too many clothes," she mumbled, as if reading his mind, and slipped her hands under the shoulders of his jacket to strip it away.

With reluctance, he pulled himself away from her glorious breasts, away from the heat between her legs, but only long enough to ditch his scratchy, ill-fitting jacket. The T-shirt he wore wasn't even his; Gaby had given him a clean one of Derek's to put on, and he stripped it off and flung it over his shoulder, not even caring where it fetched up.

Melody laughed her beautiful bell-like laugh. She was sitting back with her hands on the floor and one leg cocked up, her bra hanging off her shoulder from one arm. Pink color had risen in her cheeks to compete with the darker pink of her lips.

"Like what you see?" he asked, letting a hint of a growl slip into his voice, because women seemed to like that, and he'd never wanted to please a woman like he wanted to please this one.

She nodded vigorously, her long black hair swishing around her bare shoulders. She was still wearing her glasses and he found it unendurably hot—hotter still when she leaned forward to admire his bare chest not just with her eyes, but with hands and lips and teeth. As if the sight of his bare torso had broken some dam of desire inside her, she scrambled onto him, and he met her onslaught eagerly, burying his face in her wonderful black hair. It smelled even better than it had in his dreams, perfumed with shampoo and female arousal.

When she pulled back from enthusiastically love-biting his neck, hair tousled and glasses askew, Gunnar reached to lift the glasses from her face. She shook her head. "I want to be able to see you."

"We'll smudge 'em."

"They'll clean."

He would have liked to see her eyes without them, but there would be time, he thought. There would be time to worship all of her, to learn every last inch of her body, every mole and freckle. Time to learn everywhere she liked to be touched, when she liked it fast and when she liked it slow ...

But right now he sensed her need rising to match his own. She was in his lap, curvy and eager, all but climbing him, and he desperately wanted more of her. He allowed himself to be pressed backward to the floor, catching his weight with one arm to lower them both to the old worn floorboards. Having her on top of him sent an almost unbearable spike of desire through him, but he clenched his teeth and got hold of himself. He would make this last, for both their sakes.

So he loved her breasts with mouth and hands, as she mapped his body with her lips and her nimble fingers. She undid his jeans and he helped her peel them off along with his boxers; then he stripped off her jeans and the pink cotton panties with just a hint of lace along the edge.

He was so hard he ached, and Melody moaned softly when he cupped a hand under her curls and dipped a finger into her wetness. She was straddling him, and as she started to lower herself onto the length of him, he caught her despite the craving setting him on fire and whispered, "Wait."

"I want—" she gasped.

"I know. Me too." He lowered her gently to the floor. "But I feel like the minute I get inside you, I'm gonna—Just let me make this last for you."

MELODY

Touching him, being touched by him, was all she'd dreamed of and more. She was half out of her mind with desire, and when he dipped his head between her legs and his tongue between her folds, she arched her back as if electric current flowed through her.

She was already poised on the edge of climax, and when his fingers entered her to go with the licking—first one, then two, and finally three, pressing at her inner walls—she gasped and tumbled over the edge with a sudden white-hot shock.

He gripped her hips and eased her through it, until she fell back with another gasp and he raised his head, looking pleased.

He was glorious, every inch of him perfectly chiseled and dusted with golden hair. She wanted to trace the inkwork of his tattoos, touch him everywhere, feel him all over her. Right now she was getting at least part of her wish, as he stroked her belly and hips, thrilling her in the sensitive moments just following her orgasm. His cock was still tremendously hard and large; her eyes were drawn to it, and she ached for him even as she still fluttered from her climax.

"I—I—" she stammered, struggling to pull her thought together. "But you haven't yet—"

"Women can come more than once, or so I've heard." He sounded delighted to give it a try.

"*I* never have," she protested, but to her surprise, her first climax had hardly abated her desire. She still felt eager, desperate even. She saw from his smile that he knew. By this time the intense sensitivity from her first orgasm was starting to fade, giving way to new rising urgency, and she was the one who pulled him to her, guiding him between her legs.

She cried out when he entered her, overwhelmed by sensation and need. After the first few thrusts, they rolled over, still joined together for neither wanted to break apart; it was easier, on the hard floor, to have him underneath and Melody riding him. Anyway, like this she could see him better, and she wanted to see him, even with her long hair lashing in the way.

She could feel herself rippling toward her second climax. He held her hips firmly in his strong hands as he thrust up into her, controlling speed and depth with deft thrusts even from below. She threw her head back, closing her eyes, sweat wet on her bare back; at this point she could hardly tell where he ended and she began. She only knew they were perfectly in sync, thrusting together, her hips slamming into his as he rose to meet her. *Oh yes*, she thought incoherently, *yes*—as she came again, and he did too with a low cry, their bodies melding together as mutual waves of pleasure rolled through them both.

Melody wilted onto him, draping her body over his. It took her awhile before the boneless feeling faded enough that she could have gotten up if she'd wanted to ... and some time longer before the way the hard floor was pressing into her elbow finally made her rearrange her position and roll off him, with some regret, so she could sit up and resettle her glasses on her nose. They were smudged, as Gunnar had warned, but she decided it was well worth it. Her entire body felt as if it had been filled to the brim with honey-rich warm pleasure. She reached for the nearest item of clothing, which happened to be her shirt, and cleaned her glasses on its tails.

She had to laugh, looking around at their discarded clothing crumpled on the floor and draped over the boxes. She couldn't have chosen a better place to have her mate make love to her for the first time: surrounded by her book-hoard, or at least as much of it as would fit in a single room.

Though something soft to lie on might have been a good idea. She shifted her hips to ease the hardness of the floor.

"Good for you?" Gunnar asked, looking up at her.

"Better than good." *So* much better.

His eyelashes were gold like his hair, she noticed. Smiling, she combed her fingers through his short hair and scritched her nails against his scalp. He leaned into her hand and closed his eyes.

She could taste him on her lips, and smell him on her, deliciously, as sweat dried on her body.

"You should probably go open your store again," Gunnar murmured. "Not gonna sell very many books this way."

"I don't care if I sell a single book today." And she didn't. The bookstore could stay closed. How many customers would she actually have today, anyway—two, three, four?

Gunnar opened his eyes. "No," he said seriously. "You shouldn't talk like that. The bookstore is ... it's what you do. I can see that. I never had a—what d'you call it, a calling? I never knew what I wanted to do with my life. Maybe I wouldn't have ended up in prison if I had."

"You were in prison because of your brother, from what Ben tells me."

"Yeah, but I don't think I would've been if I had loved something the way you love this. Anyway, I don't want to talk about that." He smiled up at her. "I love watching you in the bookstore. Seeing how excited you are about it."

Melody smiled and traced the corner of his lips with her fingertips. "I just wish I could get the people in this town to share some of my excitement. When I first moved here, I thought it was such an opportunity. The old bookstore was closing, so I leased the space with all the shelves already in place, and even bought a bunch of their old stock for a song. Then I found out why they went out of business. It's hard for a small town like this to support a bookstore."

"But it's worth it?" Gunnar asked.

"Oh yes. Even on the days when I hardly sell any books. Even on the days when I just sell one." She smiled reflectively, thinking of the soul-deep satisfaction of watching a customer walk out with the perfect book. She worked so hard to make sure that each customer who came in was able to find a book they'd like. It was like a game: this little girl clutching a stuffed dog might like the Clifford books in the kids' section. Perhaps the elderly widow might be interested in seeing their cozy mysteries? And sometimes people surprised her. One of her regular customers was an old guy with a long beard and overalls, who drove up every week in his rattling truck and walked out with a bag full of romance novels. She'd helped pretty teenage girls with expensive hairdos and immaculate makeup select books on gunsmithing and auto repair.

"It's like being a matchmaking service, in a way," she said slowly. "Like I'm a matchmaker between people and books. I love that. It's something you can't get if you buy your books from an online store. Especially if they aren't really sure what they want. I love talking to them and trying to figure out what kind of book would make them happiest." She smiled again, mostly to herself, tracing little circles with her fingertips on Gunnar's well-muscled chest and combing her fingers through the curling blond hair between his pecs. "You know, I never really talked to people much, before I bought the store. I was really shy. I guess I still am, but it helps a lot to have something to talk about. ... and I guess I'm talking your ear off. About books. Again."

"I love listening to you talk."

She might have thought he was just saying that, but she couldn't deny the sincerity in Gunnar's blue eyes as he gazed up at her. Moved beyond words, she leaned down to kiss him, long and slow, running his lower lip through her teeth as she pulled back.

And then she reached for her bra with a small sigh.

"Awww," Gunnar said, propping himself up on his elbows. "Back to the bookstore?"

"I ... don't know." As much as she loved running the store, it just didn't have the usual appeal today. She hadn't really taken a proper day off since she'd moved to Autumn Grove. "Would you like to see the town? Not that there's much of it to see. You'll probably get bored before we even make it all the way through the two blocks of downtown."

"With you," Gunnar said earnestly, "I could never get bored."

He actually seemed to be telling the truth about that. Melody had worried that he'd lose interest by the second antique store, but he really seemed to be interested in all of the little small-town businesses, the tiny little park by the stream, the old-fashioned lampposts.

"I've never really been in a town like this before," he explained. "To me it's like something from TV."

They held hands as they wandered down Main Street, going into any little business that caught their eye. Melody hadn't realized how little she had explored the town, either. She'd just been too busy with her new business. She'd never been inside the hardware store, or gotten an ice cream cone at Marie's Creamery Corner.

What she hadn't expected was to get stared at. Normally, she was used to being beneath notice, hiding under her gray sweaters and quiet, drab, librarian-like exterior. Coming from her father's mansion and a clan of larger-than-life dragons, not being noticed suited her just fine.

But people noticed *Gunnar*. It was probably one part "stranger!" and one part "danger!" Women with little kids crossed the street to avoid them. Even the people who Melody had gotten to know from working at the bookstore gave her little waves but didn't come over to chat.

"How dare they," she seethed as she turned away from paying for their ice cream cones. Even the young lady behind the ice cream counter had tried not to make eye contact with Gunnar and had only spoken to Melody. "How dare they *judge* you."

Gunnar shrugged his big shoulders and licked a drop of chocolate from the edge of his cone. "They're not wrong, are they?"

"They couldn't be more wrong," she said staunchly. A passing older couple gave Gunnar a nervous look, and Melody scowled back at them until they found something else to look at.

But it was sucking the joy out of the day. And it was making her think more than she wanted to about Gunnar's past and the terms of his release, which she realized she didn't actually know. Was he out of prison permanently, or only while Ben and Derek tried to recapture Nils?

"You okay?" Gunnar asked indistinctly, crunching a bite of his waffle cone.

"I'm fine." Melody sighed and applied herself to her ice cream before it melted.

"Penny for your thoughts."

Melody grimaced. "You don't want to know. I was thinking about your brother."

"Oh." He looked pensive. "I look a lot like him, you know. Did you ever, uh, have the displeasure of meeting him?"

"No. I didn't meet Derek and Gaby until after Nils was already in jail." She looked around for a trash bin to discard their crumpled, chocolate-stained napkins. "But it doesn't matter if you look like him, Gunnar. You *aren't* your brother, not in the slightest. You're nothing like him."

"Most people don't seem to believe that."

"Nobody else," she said gently, "has looked into your soul. I know you, Gunnar. I knew from the moment I looked into your eyes that you weren't dangerous, no matter what anyone else thinks. I knew you meant no harm to us. And my brother does too, or else he wouldn't have helped you get out of prison."

Gunnar grimaced. "Wish I believed that."

"What part? About you, or about Ben?"

"Either. Both. With my brother around, I *am* putting you in danger, Melody, and—"

"Hush." She silenced him with a chocolate-flavored kiss. "No, you're not. You're here to help us. And ..." She glanced around at the quiet small-town street. "I, for one, feel safer with you here than not."

"You're biased," he pointed out, but his hand wrapped around hers, his fingers strong and warm.

"Mmmm." She smiled at him, tightening her hand in his.

"Nobody's completely unbiased, you know. Maybe I'm just biased in the *right* direction. But you know what ..." She hesitated, looking him up and down.

"What?" he asked, an anxious expression crossing his face.

"I'm thinking maybe it would help if we got you some clothes that fit." Damn it. Now she felt like she was turning into Tessa, who used to nag her about her cardigans and severe hairstyles. The cardigans were going to have to be pried out of her cold dead hands (they were *comfortable*, damn it) but the way you dressed did influence how people saw you. In her case, she knew perfectly well the impression she was putting across and didn't care to change it, but if the problem—or part of the problem—was that people tended to look at Gunnar and judge him by his hair and clothes and jail tattoos, maybe giving him a makeover might help with that. It wasn't going to change minds, exactly, but at last it could make him display on the outside the qualities that she saw on the inside.

Gunnar shrugged uncomfortably. "I don't exactly have ... you know ... a lot of money. Or much at all."

"If that's the only problem, I'll be happy to buy you something." He still looked dubious. "As a present," she said. "Look, it's at least partly a present for me, too. I get to dress you up in something sexy. What's not to enjoy about that?"

Now he looked intensely nervous. "Er ... how sexy are we talking here?"

"I'm not going to put you in Speedos. How about a leather jacket or something like that?"

"Which you're going to buy ... where, exactly?"

"Uh. Hmmm." She looked around thoughtfully. He had a point; the shopping choices in downtown Autumn Grove were somewhat limited. She knew there were a Walmart and a Target in the shopping complex down the highway, but it was a bit of a drive. Her eye lit on an outdoor supply store. "Want to see what they have in there?"

"Are you sure you can afford this?" Gunnar protested as she dragged him into the store. "I mean, you're trying to start up the bookstore and everything. There's gotta be a thrift store around here."

"Trust me, I can afford it. I don't like to lean on Dad's money if I don't have to, but my family could afford to buy this whole store."

"You're rich?" Gunnar said in surprise.

Melody scowled at him. "Say it louder, why don't you."

"Sorry." He dropped his voice and glanced around. It wasn't a large store, and they were the only customers except for an old man with a Santa Claus beard looking at hip waders. "But ... you didn't mention it. I wasn't expecting ... um ...."

"Well, you know what I am. We ..." She made a gesture, trying to indicate "stuff," but Gunnar just looked confused. "We hoard."

"I know *that*, but you hoard books."

"Yeah, but Dad doesn't. Remember what you said earlier about a stash of gold? Now imagine how much of *that* you could accumulate over a couple hundred years, with sufficient determination and no particular scruples about where it comes from."

"A couple hundred—what? You're—*what*?"

"*I'm* not that old," she whispered. "Dad is, more or less. Please stop staring at me." She grabbed a flannel shirt off a rack and held it up against him. "This looks like a good fit. Want to try it on?"

"Yeah, but ... you ..." He gave up when she shoved the shirt into his arms. "Okay."

Gunnar obediently shed his ill-fitting suit jacket and began pulling on the flannel shirt over his T-shirt. Melody took advantage of the opportunity to check out the flexing of his shoulders and the rippling muscles of his back. So did the middle-aged saleslady who was putting tags on things behind the counter, Melody couldn't help noticing.

"I just don't understand," he said quietly, buttoning the shirt. "Your life must have been so different from mine. Unimaginably different. I don't know why you're bothering with—"

Melody whipped out a hand and clamped it over his mouth. He paused in mid-buttoning and gazed at her in mild confusion.

"Because you're my mate, for one thing. But also ... look, we're *not* that different, don't you understand? Okay, so I grew up in a nice house, though I bet it wasn't whatever you're imagining. Dad has a mansion, but I grew up with my mom, and she's just got a nice townhouse in a good neighborhood."

"Your mom isn't a dragon?"

"Oh no, she is a dragon. It's just that she hoards music, not money. Here, let me get the sleeves."

As she buttoned his cuffs, Gunnar said, "How does that work?"

"About like you'd imagine, I guess. She's got a million records and CDs in storage. Digital music was a godsend for our closet space. She also owns a recording studio and represents some bands. That part kind of comes and goes, because on the one hand, being a patron and muse for her own band is her dream life, but she's also somewhat on the unreliable end of things, and she's not actually that good at finding bands who are going to do *well*. Mostly they're a money sink. But she has fun and does some charity work, like organizing benefit concerts, and that sort of thing."

"That's ..." Gunnar shook his head. "That's not what I was expecting. At all."

Melody smiled. "We're all different, just like anybody. Anyway, I grew up in a modest townhouse because Mom always sunk her money into her hobby, the same way Dad likes to hold onto his and invest it in precious things. Turn around."

Gunnar rotated obediently. "You like this one?" he asked with a hopeful little smile.

"I do, but I'm not really feeling the lumberjack plaid ..."

I t was hours later when they left the store, Gunnar freshly decked out in a new flannel shirt with creases so crisp that he kept squirming, and Melody carrying the bag with his old clothes.

He looked, if she did say so herself, amazing. She would've preferred maybe a little more 5th Avenue and less backwoods chic, but at least these clothes fit him and flattered him, unlike the old brown suit. The lumberjack look was hot on him. She'd found him a dark gray work jacket, which he was wearing over a shirt in a subdued green and gray checked pattern.

And it was fascinating how the clothes changed the way he fit into his environment. Suddenly, rather than looking like a stranger who might easily be fresh out of prison, he just looked like someone who was maybe down from one of the logging camps up in the mountains, or a local farmer. People no longer crossed the street to avoid him. Instead there were friendly smiles and curious glances. An older couple even stopped to congratulate her on her young man and ask for Gunnar's name. Melody was blushing fiercely by the time they moved on.

But Gunnar seemed pensive, subdued even. "Doesn't it

seem fake to you?" he asked quietly. "They wouldn't have given me the time of day before."

"They just don't know what to think of you. This helps. It's like camouflage; it lets you blend into a crowd."

He touched a hand to the side of her face. "Is that what you do?"

She didn't pretend not to know what he was talking about. "Look, it's complicated. My father wants me to be ... ornamental, I guess. Beautiful and deadly."

"You are beautiful, no matter what," Gunnar said softly. He smiled. "And probably deadly too."

"It doesn't bother you?" she asked. Although there was no one nearby on the sidewalk, she lowered her voice. "Knowing what I am."

"Why should it? If you're not afraid of *me*, knowing what *I* am ... why would I be afraid of you?" He leaned in to sip at her lips, and murmured, "I would like to see your dragon sometime, though."

Her heart fluttered. No one had ever seen her shift except other dragons, and more recently, Ben and Tessa—but that was due to necessity: she'd had to fight another dragon to protect them. She had never just shifted because someone wanted to see her do it before.

"Wait until dark. I'll show you then—" Her phone inter-rupted her with an incoming text. She rolled her eyes when she saw who it was. "It's Ben, checking up on us."

Gunnar grinned. "You gonna tell him what we were up to?"

"And have him go all protective big brother on me? Hell no." She typed a brief return text letting him know she was still with Gunnar, still in Autumn Grove, and doing abso-lutely fine. "I told him I was showing you the town."

"Well, that's not wrong. Though ..." He glanced around. "I kinda think we've seen most of it."

BEAR IN A BOOKSHOP

"In that case, I suggest we get something to eat." She swept a hand down the line of shopfronts. "As you can see, you have your choice of diner food or ... diner food. There's also a biker bar up by the highway, and some chain restaurants out where the Target and all of that is, but it's a little bit of a drive."

Gunnar's stomach rumbled, and he flashed a quick, embarrassed grin. "Diner food sounds great."

GUNNAR

They got a late lunch at a diner with checked red-and-white tablecloths and a waitress who knew Melody's name. This whole place was like something out of a movie, Gunnar thought. He kept plucking at the sleeves of his new shirt. He didn't know how to feel about any of it.

The one thing he was sure about was that it didn't really matter where he was as long as Melody was with him. She pressed her knee against his under the table, and they lingered over coffee long after their burgers were gone, talking about anything and everything and nothing. She told him about growing up with an emotionally distant record-producer mother—they left the dragon thing unspoken due to the risk of eavesdroppers as the café began to fill up with the dinner crowd—and he talked about growing up with Nils.

"He took care of me after our parents died. He was really all I had. I can't blame everything that went wrong in my life on Nils, it really isn't fair—"

"It seems fair enough to me," Melody said stubbornly. "He's the whole reason you were in prison in the first place."

"Yeah, but I made a lot of mistakes all on my own. Like I said, I never really knew what I wanted to do with my life. Even after I decided I didn't want to follow in Nils's footsteps, I still just ... drifted. Worked as a bar bouncer, moved crates in a warehouse, took on some construction jobs, that kind of thing. I kept feeling like I wanted to do something else with my life, anything else, but I never could figure out *what*."

"Well, what are you interested in?" Melody asked. "If you could do anything, anything at all—if money didn't matter—what would you like to do?"

If money didn't matter. For her, of course, it didn't. For him, scraping by at jobs that were minimum wage or temporary or seasonal—or all three—life had always been a lot more uncertain. He'd sometimes wished that it was a hundred years ago, when a guy like him could just jump on a tramp steamer headed for unknown ports. These days, getting the good union-wage jobs that might lead to a life like that wasn't easy. Even joining the Army wasn't open to him, with his criminal background and lack of a high school education.

So he'd tried not to fantasize about a life he couldn't have. He just kicked around from one dead-end job to another. He'd thought that if you didn't have dreams, you couldn't be disappointed.

But now he was starting to realize that if you didn't have dreams, you couldn't achieve them, either. Dreams were a map of the future. You might not make it to every point on the map, but without a map, you'd never get anywhere at all.

"I think I'd like to travel. I've never really been much of anywhere." As soon as the words left his mouth, he instantly regretted them. Melody was clearly not a traveling type. With all the money in the world to do whatever *she* wanted, she'd settled down in a small town and started a bookstore. He might as well have just flat-out said *I'm planning to skip out on you.* Except that wasn't what he'd meant at all. Floundering desperately for something else, he grabbed at straws. "And ... uh ... finish my GED? I'm pretty close. I've been working on it in prison—" Oh great, there he went, talking about prison again. *Thanks, mouth.*

But her face was open, unjudging. "I can help you with that last part," she said. "We have study guides and that kind of thing. I've helped other people do it. There's not a library in Autumn Grove, it's too small, so I try to fill some of the functions with my bookstore that people might go to a library for. And I am absolutely dead serious about helping you get tested for dyslexia, too."

"And you wouldn't mind all that work?"

She brushed the side of her hand along his. "Stop acting like it's some terrible burden for me to spend time with you, Gunnar. I *like* spending time with you."

"Same here," he murmured, closing his hand around hers.

Melody beckoned the waitress for a refill on her coffee. "You know," she said gently, when the waitress had gone to help another customer. "I think I'd like to hear about prison. What it was like for you."

Gunnar shook his head vigorously. The last thing he wanted was to expose his mate—his soft, beautiful mate—to the experiences he'd gone through. "No, you don't. It's not a nice place, definitely not something you'd want to know about."

"Oh, come on. I'm not that fragile."

"It's not because I think you're fragile, it's because there are some things *most* people don't want to hear about, and prison life is one of 'em."

"Did you know my dad is a mobster?" Melody asked

conversationally, stirring a packet of sweetener into her coffee.

"... what?"

"Oh, he doesn't *call* it that. But that's what it amounts to. I told you my dad's rich and he's not especially scrupulous about where the money comes from. You might have been thinking 'shady business deals' when I said that, but it's a lot more than that. I used to help him keep the books, so I know how many pies he's got a finger in. You said prison isn't nice; well, neither is my dad, and neither are a lot of the people he deals with."

Gunnar sat back in his chair and looked at her with new appreciation. His entire view of her had just tilted on its side. The sweet little bookworm was a dragon mob princess. What a weird world.

"Why didn't you tell me earlier? I thought I had to be so careful around you ..." He laughed out loud; he couldn't help it. "Hell, if you used to be a mob accountant, you could probably teach *me* a thing or two about the shadier side of the world."

Melody turned pink and looked around hastily. "I wasn't a —a mob accountant! I just helped Dad with his—oh, shit." It was the first time he'd heard her swear. "You're right. I was."

He was full-on grinning now, probably showing every one of his teeth. "I can't believe it. You look so sweet."

"I *am* sweet!" Melody protested, crossing her arms over her librarian cardigan. That didn't help much; from Gunnar's point of view, it just drew his attention to the curves filling out the soft gray fabric underneath her clamped arms.

"Never said you weren't."

Her blush flamed hotter. "I shouldn't have told you."

Gunnar set down his coffee cup and reached quickly across the table to rest his hands on her arms. Melody reluctantly unkinked her arms and let him take her hands in his.

"I'm glad you did," he said sincerely, looking into her eyes. "I thought we didn't have anything in common at first. But we do. We both like books, even if we don't like the same books. And I don't have to be careful with you, not like I thought. You're tougher than you look. Dragon scales under the skin."

Her coral-rose mouth curved in a reluctant smile. "I'd still like it if you'd be a *little* careful with me."

The words were demure, but libido stirred in him again. He wanted to lay her out on soft white sheets, not just make love to her in the back room of a bookstore ... pamper her like she deserved to be pampered.

"Always," he promised, reaching to touch her cheek.

Melody leaned her face into his hand like a petted cat; then she blinked, looking out the window behind him. "It's getting dark out there. How long have we been in here?"

"Awhile, I guess." He glanced out at the dark street, lit with iron lampposts that looked like something out of an old photo. "Is there anywhere to have fun around here?"

"Fun?" Melody said, as if she'd never heard of the concept.

"Yeah, you know. Dancing, or ... fun."

"I don't know. Since I got here, I've mostly just been busy with the bookstore. When I have free time, I—"

"—read," he finished for her.

"Yes," she said, blushing again. "There's the biker bar, but that's all I know about locally. Anyway, I guess we should be getting back to the farm before Ben comes to drag us back."

"You want to?"

"No," she admitted, curling her fingers in his hands. Her eyes glimmered with mischief. "What do you think they'll do to us if we stay out past curfew?"

"You want to find out?" He was grinning again. "Ever been to a biker bar?"

"I don't want to go to a biker bar!" Suddenly her eyes lit

up. "You know what we *can* do, though. Remember that thing I said I'd show you after dark? I think it's getting dark enough."

His heart flipped over. In his chest, his bear stirred. "Yeah. I'd love to see that."

Melody left cash on the table, including a more-than-generous tip, and they went out hand in hand into the evening. The sky was still deep blue rather than black, painted with dying sunset colors over the mountains. The air was warm and fragrant.

He expected Melody to go back to the bookstore and her car, but instead they walked down Main Street past a gas station and a closed auto repair place. Beyond that, the town petered out into fields and woods.

Gunnar slowed, clutching at Melody's hand.

"What?" she asked him, looking up at him, startled.

"Fireflies," he breathed.

They were everywhere out here, dancing in the dusk. The edge of the woods was full of them.

"Haven't you seen them before?"

"A few, here and there, in parks, but not often. I'm a city kid, remember?" He stared around in wonder. The town wasn't far—he could hear the traffic on the highway—but it felt like they were completely alone. There were no house lights anywhere in sight, nothing but the glimmer of the fireflies, like a whirling dance of captive stars.

Melody took off her glasses. Without them, her eyes looked huge. "Hold these for me. And ... this." She hesitated briefly before slipping the necklace over her head and placing it carefully into his hand.

He wanted to ask what was inside the locket—as tenderly as she handled it, whatever it was must mean a lot to her—but she was already walking away from him, into the field.

"Wait," he called. "Aren't you going to take off the rest of your clothes? I, uh—I can hold them for you too."

Melody turned around. She pulled the pins out of her hair and it unfurled like a black flag, tumbling over her shoulders. "Since I'm a dragon, my clothes shift with me," she said, tucking the pins into her pocket. "But jewelry and accessories don't, unless they're in a pocket. I have no idea how it works."

"That's convenient, though, about the clothes." He tried not to show his disappointment; he'd been looking forward to watching her get undressed.

"I know. It's handy." She clasped her hands in front of herself. "Ready? Make sure no one's coming."

"It's just us," he breathed. She was a vision in the dusk, painted in shades of black and gray and white, surrounded by fireflies. Her hair flowed around her in an inky cascade. He had to talk her into wearing it down more.

Melody bowed her head and closed her eyes.

Her shift was a rippling, flowing thing. She didn't change so much as *poured* into her new shape. A torrent of silver flowed from her, lengthening into her dragon's long neck and delicate head with two curving horns, expanding into a pair of great wings arching above her back.

Her dragon was silver, with deep gray eyes flecked with gold. As she stood looking down at him, Gunnar felt his bear straining inside his chest, wanting to burst out and hunt with her in the dark woods. He couldn't help thinking what a striking pair they'd make, his white polar-bear fur and her silver scales.

But they hadn't both agreed to shift, and someone had to stay human to deal with passers-by. They were too close to town for Gunnar to feel comfortable shifting. People might catch a glimpse of a dragon and write it off as a hallucination; everyone knew dragons didn't exist. An enormous white bear was a different story.

"Well?" Melody asked, and he jumped. "What do you think?"

"I didn't know you could talk as a dragon! I can't talk as a bear."

She laughed softly. If her human voice was musical, her voice as a dragon was a dozen times more so, different harmonics layered over each other until it was like an orchestra had tuned itself into the approximate cadence of human speech. Her name had never seemed so appropriate.

"Like the clothes thing," she said in that magical, musical voice, "it's another thing we can do that most shifters can't. Unless you're a parrot shifter or something."

Captivated, he stepped forward. "May I touch you?"

"Please," Melody said softly, lowering her long, slender head.

He placed a hand carefully on the side of her face. She closed her eyes in bliss, and he stroked her. She was warm to the touch; somehow he'd expected her to be cool. The skin around her lips was very soft. As he ran his hand along the side of her face, the soft skin changed to the dry, warm texture of her scales. He rubbed under her jaw and felt her pulse beating beneath the fine, overlapping scales on her neck.

"Melody," he said, and she opened her eyes. "You ever take passengers?"

She blinked slowly. "I ... think I could do that. I've never tried. I know my father can."

She folded her legs beneath her, lying down so he could mount easily. After carefully tucking her glasses and locket into the pocket of his jacket, he climbed onto her back, while she twisted her head around on her long, supple neck to watch his progress. She held her wings low to the ground, half folded, to keep them out of the way.

"Is this comfortable?" Gunnar asked, settling his legs just in front of her wings. She was firm and muscular between his legs; he tried not to think too hard about that. It was human-Melody he pictured, not dragon-Melody, but in either case, getting a raging hard-on while riding a dragon seemed like a bad idea.

"It feels fine," she said. "You can hold onto my spikes."

She had a row of hornlike protrusions marching down her spine, stopping just above the shoulders where he was clinging on. Gunnar gingerly gripped two of them. "No chance I'm gonna hurt you?"

"I don't think so. I'll let you know."

She stood up carefully and gave herself a little shake. The scales rippled under him like the fur on the back of a cat. "Ready?"

"Ready." He hoped his voice didn't sound as tight to her as it did to him.

"If you fall, I'll catch you," Melody promised. She beat down, hard, flattening the grass in a rippling circle around them.

It took a lot of flapping to get them airborne—Melody herself looked pretty heavy in this form, and Gunnar wasn't a small guy. For a minute or two, he thought they weren't going to get off the ground at all. Then she seemed to find the rhythm of it; he felt the wind catch them, and suddenly they were above the trees, going up in a rising spiral.

Gunnar clenched tighter on her spikes.

"Okay back there?" Melody asked, twisting her head around. It didn't seem to interfere with her flying.

"No worries." It came out breathless; he managed to steady his voice. "You?"

"Just fine."

He could see the town now, the lampposts and the streets they'd just walked down; he could see the flicker of head-lights on the highway. Melody continued to climb, her strong downbeats driving them higher in the night sky. Beneath his legs, her muscles flexed rhythmically, holding them both up with seeming effortlessness. He wasn't sure if it felt the same way to fly as it did to swim, but he was reminded of the handful of times, in his urban polar bear existence, when he'd managed to go night-swimming in a lake or harbor. Perhaps someday he'd get to go swimming in the ocean.

The cool night air flowed like water over him. He drew it deep into his lungs. Above them, the stars seemed very sharp and clear.

"Are you comfortable?" Melody asked. She circled in a great wide sweep. "Too cold?"

"No, I'm fine." He looked down past her wings, and slowly his death-grip on her spines began to ease. She was right, she'd catch him if he fell. It surprised him to find that he trusted her to do that.

And I'll catch you too, he promised her silently. *Always.*

"Do you want to go somewhere?" she asked. "It seems like a shame to come up and just land again."

With the night wind flowing through his hair, Gunnar turned his face toward the distant glow of city lights in the night, and grinned. "Hey, you got to give me a makeover today, and took me flying. How about I take you dancing at somewhere nicer than a biker bar?"

There was a hesitation, just long enough to make him worry, and then he heard the smile in her voice as she turned her head toward the city. "I'd love to."

A t first they flew over a dark ocean of trees, with the scattered lights of houses below. As the houses and the roads grew denser, Melody angled for the dark, coiling loops of the river cutting through the countryside. She skimmed upriver with her wingtips almost touching the dark water, and came in for a neat landing on a stretch of unlit access road beside a pier. Gunnar slid off her back an instant before she collapsed back to her human form.

"Done this before?" he remarked.

She smiled. "My favorite flying is usually with my father on his estate, because we don't have to hide there. But don't forget, I grew up as an urban dragon. I know all the tricks for flying in the city. It's easier to hide in bad weather, such as rain or snow. But not nearly as comfortable for a passenger. Could I get my things back, please?"

Gunnar handed back her glasses and the locket. "You got any preferences about where to go?" he asked as she fastened the locket around her neck. "Got any favorite clubs or bars?"

She laughed. God, he loved her laugh. "I'm not exactly the nightclubbing type. For that matter, neither of us is dressed for clubbing right now."

She'd left her hair down. Gunnar ran his fingers through the silky black strands. "You want to do some more clothes shopping?" he asked. He'd never thought he might actually *want* to go shopping for clothes, especially after spending an interminable time at it earlier that day, but now he was picturing Melody in a dancing dress—dark red to complement her black-and-white coloring, or silver like her dragon, hugging her curves and rippling around her when she moved ...

Melody caught his hand and laced her fingers through his. "I think we're fine as we are. We'll set a new trend."

MELODY

She was having the time of her life.

Melody had never really been interested in the nightlife scene before. In college, she'd gone out clubbing a few times with Tessa or other friends, as one did. And she'd had dates take her dancing once or twice, and had occasionally gone out for drinks after work with Tessa. But in general, as she'd told Gunnar, she preferred to stay in with a book in the evening.

Now she understood why people liked this sort of thing. For her, it was all about the company.

Gunnar grinned at her and she grinned back as she danced to a fast techno beat, her unbound hair swirling around her. She'd stripped off her cardigan long ago—she wasn't even sure where it had gotten off to, or if she'd accidentally left it behind at the last place, and she didn't really care. A couple of fruity mixed drinks were humming in her system, but not enough to make her drunk, just enough to give the world a soft golden edge and fill her with euphoria.

She had been right that they stood out. Even without the cardigan, she was still wearing her modest button-up white shirt that she was well aware looked like the kind of thing a teacher would wear. Gunnar's crisp new work shirt was, surprisingly, *not* the only flannel she'd seen all evening—there were a few people around, both men and women, sporting a sort of retro lumberjack look—but it was a whole different thing when combined with work pants rather than skinny jeans and man-buns.

But Melody couldn't care less, and Gunnar didn't seem to care either. In fact, she'd be surprised if he'd noticed anything else in this nightclub except for her. His beer was largely untouched. He only seemed to have eyes for her, and he didn't seem to care if the DJ was playing slow songs, fast songs, or any kind of song that either of them had heard before; he wanted to be out on the dance floor with her.

The song ended and she plunked, sweaty and buzzed and happy, into her seat and picked up her half-empty drink, looking at it under the club's colored lights. Most of the ice was melted. It was hot in here.

"Get you another?" Gunnar asked over the cheerful noise of the crowd.

Melody shook her head. "Not right now. I don't drink much. No sense drinking myself under the table." She leaned forward and smiled at him. "I want to—"

She broke off when Gunnar's face changed very suddenly. He was looking at something behind her.

Her first, panicked thought was *Nils?*, especially when she looked around to see people on the nightclub floor parting in a wave. Then the crowd cleared enough that she could see her brother storming toward them. He looked absolutely furious.

Gunnar started to get up, noticed Melody was remaining seated, and stayed uncomfortably in his chair as Ben loomed over them, scowling.

"What are you two doing here?" he asked, his voice a little too calm.

"Dancing," Melody said. "As if it's any of your business."

"Actually," Gunnar said awkwardly, not looking at either of them, "it kind of is."

"Yeah, seeing as I'm his parole officer," Ben said. "Bad life choices aside, it's not like I can stop *you* from doing what you want to do, but I can certainly stop him. And you weren't answering your phone."

"I put it on silent because I didn't want to be *interrupted*," Melody said pointedly. Ben continued to loom, failing to take the hint. "How'd you find us?"

"Called in a couple favors from old buddies on the force and tracked your phone. You realize, with Nils out there, how it's going to look to everyone else if you just vanish and don't turn up at the farm after work, right?"

It finally managed to penetrate her annoyance that, underneath *his* annoyance, Ben looked really freaked out.

"Okay, so it was impulsive," she admitted. "But, look, we're fine, as you can clearly see. We were just going to do some dancing and then come back. I refuse to live my life under house arrest."

Ben pointed to Gunnar. "He is *literally* under house arrest. You realize that, right?"

Now Melody stood up. The thing that irritated her most was knowing that Ben did kind of, sort of, have a point. "What was I supposed to do, ask your permission?"

"You could at least have told me where you were going!"

"At which point you would have said no, and we'd have fought, and I'd have done it anyway except I'd be mad and wouldn't enjoy it as much. What's the point of that?"

Ben's eyebrows had been steadily climbing upward until she reached the end of her mini-rant. Turning to Gunnar, he said, "I'd just like to point out that she used to never argue with anyone, including me. It looks like she's found her assertive side. Lucky you."

"I like her that way," Gunnar said with a grin that, Melody thought, would probably have looked casual if you didn't know him. He was very tense. Still, she appreciated the support.

"Apparently so," Ben sighed. Then his gaze sharpened, going between the two of them. That was his "detective" look. "You two got awfully close, awfully quick. Tell me, sis, is this just casual dating, or something more?"

Melody was frozen on the edge of a reply. Ben could usually tell when people were lying; years of practice had made his panther highly attuned to nuance. And she wasn't even sure she *wanted* to lie, not anymore, not about this.

But before she could open her mouth and tell him the truth, Ben's phone buzzed audibly in his pocket. He raised his hand and stepped away. "Yeah?"

Whatever was being said on the other end of the line made visible shock and alarm go through him like a livewire. "Are you hurt?" he asked sharply. "Is the baby okay? Is *everyone* okay?"

Gunnar was on his feet now. He exchanged a look with Melody, who shook her head helplessly.

"I've found Mel, so we'll be there as soon as possible," Ben said. "I love you." He hung up the phone and turned to the other two. Taking a deep breath, eyes fixed on Gunnar, he said, "Your brother just attacked Derek and Gaby's farm."

~

Flying to the farm with two people on her back was a lot more exhausting than with one, but it was faster than taking Ben's car, and Melody wasn't about to leave Gunnar behind. Half an hour ago, she would happily have left *Ben* behind, but her sisterly annoyance had faded away like snow in the summer sun when things had turned deadly serious.

She hadn't realized until now that some part of her, a rather large part of her, had believed Nils was never going to show up. She'd honestly thought her brother was being paranoid. If *she* was on the run from the law, she certainly wouldn't head for the first place they'd look! She had assumed that Nils was probably headed for a different country as fast as he could go, and they'd deal with extra security on the farmhouse for a week or two, then go back to their normal lives.

Foolish. Naive.

Ben said that nobody was hurt, but she still pushed her wings as fast as she could beat them, and didn't start to relax until she circled over the farmhouse. The house and yard blazed with lights, an electric wall holding back the dark. Melody glided in for a landing on the open lawn next to where the cars were parked. Derek came down from the porch to meet them, carrying a shotgun, as Melody shifted back and retrieved her glasses and necklace from Gunnar.

As he approached, Derek swung the shotgun to point at Gunnar.

"Knock it off," Ben said shortly, pushing the muzzle away. "He was with Melody the whole time."

"They could be contacting each other somehow," Derek said gruffly.

"He's not a traitor," Melody flared. "Like Ben said, he was with me all day. What happened?"

Derek let out a breath. "Let's get in the house and I'll fill you in. After that, now that you're back, one of us needs check the perimeter. I didn't want to leave the women alone in the house."

The tension was contagious, and Melody felt something

inside her ease as the door closed behind them and Ben locked it. The rest of the household was clustered in the living room, Gaby with a sleepy Sandy in her arms and her mother holding the baby. Tessa had been sitting beside Gaby, but she jumped up and came running to hug Melody, pregnant belly bumping awkwardly between them. "Melody! I was so worried when we couldn't find you! Thank God you're okay."

Tessa's obvious worry made her feel guilty in a way that getting chewed out by her brother hadn't. "I'm sorry, Tess. I just wanted to get away for a little while."

"What happened?" Gunnar asked in his deep, quiet voice.

Derek gave him a hard look. It was Tessa who answered.

"We think he was mainly testing our defenses rather than making a serious attempt to get inside. Something tripped the security system, and when Derek went out to check it, Ghost—Nils—whatever you want to call him tried to get in at the back door."

Ben sucked in his breath, and Derek glowered.

"What did you do?" Melody asked, glancing toward the kitchen. Its lights were on, like every other light in the house, and she could see that the back door—leading to the back deck, where she'd just that morning had coffee with Gunnar —had been boarded up.

"Tessa drove him off with an axe," Gaby said admiringly.

Tessa flushed. "You make it sound like a bigger deal than it was. I grabbed an axe that we use to chop up wood for the fireplace, and ran into the kitchen just as the door broke in and swung it at his face."

All three of the new arrivals were now staring at her. "No big *deal*?" Melody repeated. Ben put an arm around his hugely pregnant wife and kissed her.

"I just swung at his face and missed, though," Tessa protested, blushing hotter under the dark-caramel tint of her

BEAR IN A BOOKSHOP

skin. "I was yelling, and Gaby was yelling, and Derek heard us and came running with the shotgun. By that time Nils was gone."

"Are you sure it was him?" Gunnar asked quietly, his big hands clenching into fists.

"He was shifted," Tessa said, "so, yes, unless there are a lot of polar bears around this part of the country."

"That decides it, though," Derek said. "It's not safe here. We need to move the family somewhere safe."

"Darius," Tessa said promptly. "He'll help us, I'm sure."

Ben made a faint protesting noise, but subsided. "You're right," he said, looking subdued. "I can call him."

Tessa shook her head. "I can do it. If we need is a safe place to go for a few days, I'm sure he'll let us stay with him."

Gaby looked uncertain. "Are you sure we'll be safer in the home of a dragon mob—er—" She glanced down at Sandy, who seemed to have fallen asleep in her arms, but still changed directions with the sentence. "I'm not sure we'll be safer there than here."

"Neither am I," Melody said. In her entire lifetime, she couldn't remember her dad ever having human guests, aside from that one time Ben had showed up with Tessa in tow and hadn't really given him a choice.

However, Tessa and her father seemed to have an unusual rapport. She wished *she* could get her dad to listen to her the way he listened to the small woman with all the cats.

"Yeah, I'm kinda with Melody on that," Derek said. "There's no need to call your dragon in-laws. We can arrange a safehouse. Probably should've done it already. My fault. I thought we'd be able to hold him off better here, but this place just isn't defensible enough."

"What on earth could be safer than a mansion guarded by a dragon?" Tessa asked. "It'll do good for Darius to have some company for a change. He can get used to having kids around before he has to deal with actual grandchildren."

Melody and Ben exchanged a look of mutual dismay, sharing a moment of sibling same-wavelength rapport. "Honey, Dad is *terrible* with kids," Ben said. "Including his own."

"*Especially* his own," Melody muttered.

"Well, that's why he needs practice," Tessa said brightly, taking out her phone.

The soft clunk of the door closing jerked Melody away from the conversation. She spun around, realizing that Gunnar was no longer with them.

"Gunnar!" She ran to the now-unlocked door and opened it. Ben appeared instantly at her elbow, reaching for his shoulder holster.

The porch was empty as Melody ran out onto it, but there at the top of the steps was a pile of discarded clothing. She couldn't tell if it was just her imagination that she thought she saw a flash of white at the far side of the pasture.

"Gunnar!" she shouted into the night.

"Damn it," Ben murmured. Melody turned as he holstered his gun. "Sorry, sis. Looks like they were in cahoots the whole time."

"They certainly were *not!*" She spun around, straining her eyes as she scanned the woods for another elusive flash of white. "He's going to try to find Nils and stop him. I'm sure he is. *Damn* it! We can't let him go alone."

"What the hell is the deal with you and this guy, Mel?" Ben asked.

"He's my *mate*, you idiot," she snapped.

The words fell into a sudden silence. She was all too aware of Derek and Tessa in the doorway, Gaby behind them. Not that she'd really *planned* how she wanted to tell them, but this sure wasn't it.

Derek cleared his throat. "Are ... you sure?"

This caused everyone else, Gaby in particular, to give him a disbelieving stare.

"Right. Yes. Forget I said anything."

"Melody ..." Ben was looking at her with open worry now, fumbling for words. "I know what it feels like, when you look into someone else's heart like that. I know what it feels like when you think you've found your other half—"

"What do you mean, *when I think*?" she flared. "You've found *your* mate; you *know* what it feels like. You wanted to know why I'm so sure that there's no harm in Gunnar? It's because I can see his *soul*. Like he can see mine. And the longer we argue about this, the longer he's in danger, all alone, trying to protect us all."

She could see they didn't believe her. Even Ben didn't seem to believe her, and he should know better. Tessa had been her best friend since high school, but she wasn't a shifter; she didn't *know*, in the bone-deep way that shifters knew.

Melody turned away. "Fine," she said, storming down the steps. "I'll find him on my own."

"Melody!" Ben called, but she was already shifting. The change came more violently than her usual transformations, her dragon erupting out of her with pent-up fury. She didn't remember about her glasses until they fell off her nose. The chain on the locket was stretched tight around her scaly, silver throat, but not tightly enough to break.

Oh well. For perhaps the first time in her life, she didn't care. If no one picked up her glasses, she had a spare pair back in her apartment.

The important thing was to find Gunnar before he found Nils, and got himself killed.

She beat her wings and took off with a hard downdraft, soaring into the night sky.

GUNNAR

Gunnar ran through the dark woods, his bear's legs pumping in time with the beating of his powerful heart, following the traces of Nils's scent.

He shouldn't have just run off without saying anything to Melody; he knew that. But every moment he waited was a moment when Nils was getting farther away. And, anyway, the only thing he'd get if he explained what he had in mind was endless arguments. Arguments from Melody's brother and friends, who didn't trust him; arguments from Melody, who would worry about him.

No, Nils was *his* problem to deal with. That had always been true, ever since they were young.

Last time, he'd given Nils the benefit of the doubt. And he'd gone to prison for it. This time, he had people to protect. Gunnar intended to put his own flesh and fur, claws and teeth, between Melody and Nils. If his brother threatened one hair on her head, one scale on her body—and a threat to her family might as well be a threat to Melody herself; he knew that by now—

Nils was going to regret the day he messed with the Keegan family.

Gunnar's bear didn't seem to care; his bear was simply thrilled to be out and running, relishing the smells and sounds of the dark forest. Even before prison, as an urban bear, he'd rarely gotten to enjoy this kind of freedom. He wished he *could* just enjoy it, without the human side of him being acutely distracted by the confrontation to come.

As he pursued the fresh, hot trail of Nils's familiar scent deeper into the woods, he began to cross other, older trails. Older by days, older by weeks—Nils must have been living back here since he'd escaped prison. Which, now that Gunnar thought about it, made all the sense in the world. They had been thinking in human terms, as if Nils were an ordinary escaped convict, making lists of his old contacts and known bolt holes and ways that he might try to get out of the country. Even Gunnar had been thinking that way.

But Nils didn't have to do any of that. All he had to do was shift into a bear, and he could live in the mountains indefinitely. A polar bear this far south was pretty conspicuous, but he had a human mind to drive his bear's habits. He could stay out of sight, feed himself by hunting, and live comfortably off the land as long as he wanted.

Gunnar suspected he might have thought of it earlier if he hadn't spent his entire life in the city. But Nils hadn't. Nils had been all over the world, working as a gun for hire on nearly every continent. He had plenty of experience at surviving in the wilderness, as a bear or a human.

And if you'd just taken off and decided to make your home in a different forest, you could have lived there for years, with no one guessing a thing, Gunnar thought angrily in his brother's direction.

But no, Nils had to come back seeking revenge on the people who'd put him in prison and their mates. And now,

Gunnar and Nils were headed toward a clash that had probably been coming for a long time, maybe their entire lives.

As Gunnar ran, his childhood memories kept pace with him, surfacing in his mind in bright flashes. He remembered good times and bad ones. Memories of Nils mercilessly bullying him. Nils showing him how to hotwire his first car. Nils making sure there were groceries in the house, or the two of them playing together as small children ...

There had been a lot of childhood cruelty that Nils had made sure their mother never saw: stealing or breaking Gunnar's toys, pushing him down in the sandbox. But there had also been times when they played together happily, wrestling and laughing as little children do. And Gunnar truly believed that all the things Nils had taught him as a teenager—how to shoplift and steal cars, how to forge rent checks—had been well intentioned, if terribly misguided. Nils had believed that it was a harsh, cruel world out there, and everything he had taught Gunnar were survival skills for the world as Nils thought it was.

"You have to get them before they get you," he'd said.

And: *"All we've got is each other, kid. We have to look out for each other."*

Bears couldn't weep, but Gunnar felt the ghostly prickle of tears in his eyes anyway. He wanted *that* brother back, the brother he'd glimpsed in those rare soft moments in between all the harshness and cruelty and anger ... the brother who, he now suspected, had never really existed except in his own childhood idolization of his adored older sibling. Certainly, Nils had not been that person for many years.

All we've got is each other.

But that wasn't true anymore, was it? Into the home-movie reel of childhood memories, something new began to intrude: memories of Melody. The softness of her hair, the warmth of her laugh, the sparkle in her gray eyes. The subtle strength as her fingers curled around his. The way she defended him against her family, and listened when he talked.

They had both misjudged each other in the beginning. Like most people, she hadn't been able to see past his bruiser looks and jail tattoos—but he was no better; he'd failed to see the strength underlying her soft-looking surface. She wouldn't hurt and abandon him like Nils had. This was a mate who would stand by him no matter what the world threw at them.

Gunnar slowed. Nils's scent was very fresh now. The trail had led him away from the hilly farmland around Autumn Grove into the mountains. It was possible one of the other shifters at the farmhouse might follow their scent the same way Gunnar had followed Nils's, but if so, they had a head start; they'd have at least a few minutes before anyone bothered them.

From the rocks ahead of him came a low growl. The wind brought him Nils's scent, fresh and strong.

Gunnar bristled as his bear surged inside him, wanting to fight. Unlike Gunnar's human mind, his bear wasn't restrained by memories of their childhood. His bear knew that Nils was a threat, not a fellow cub anymore, but another big boar bear to fight.

Gunnar shifted so he could speak. "Come out where I can see you. I know you're there."

Even as a human, his slightly-sharper-than-usual senses could pick up Nils's scent. There was a faint sliver of moon in the clear sky, just enough to lace Nils's white fur with silver as the other polar bear strolled into view, his muscles rippling beneath his shaggy hide.

Gunnar had forgotten how enormous Nils was. Scars from other fights slashed through Nils's pale coat, trophies of old fights won—and, Gunnar guessed, one fight lost, against Derek Ruger.

That was what Nils could not forgive. He might not even mind the prison sentence so much as losing a fight to another bear. He'd never been able to back down or walk away.

Are you any better? Gunnar asked himself.

He shook off the doubts. Unlike Nils, he hadn't chosen this fight. He was here to defend, not to attack.

"I went to prison because of you," he said quietly.

Nils shifted abruptly into his human form, huge and muscular. His hair was longer now than he'd kept it when Gunnar had known him, a tangled blond mess full of leaves, and he had several weeks' scruff of a beard. "Am I supposed to apologize?" His voice was rough from disuse.

"It'd be a start, yes."

"A start on what? Renewing our brotherly bonds?" Nils sneered. "You made it clear how you feel about me when you took their side and threw in with that bunch of cowards and mixed shifters down the hill."

"They're not your enemies."

"*Everyone* is the enemy! Didn't I teach you anything? The only person you can trust in this world is yourself. Take them out before they take you out. That's how it works."

Gunnar shook his head slowly. "That's not how most people are. That's just how *you* are. It doesn't have to be that way."

"Yeah? Well, if you believe in our brotherly unity so much, then join me." Nils grinned fiercely, his teeth flashing white. "We'll attack them together. Between the two of us, I bet we can take that bear and panther, even their dragon watchdog."

Gunnar recoiled in horror. "I'd rather die!"

"Then you will," Nils growled, his words distorting as he shifted.

Gunnar shifted too. He met the other bear with a clash that shook the trees.

They hadn't ever fought, *truly* fought. They'd wrestled as kids, but in the half-serious, half-playful way that brothers always fought. As a younger man, Gunnar had brawled with other large-predator shifters like himself, out back of shifter bars, but those fights had been nothing more than drunk, rowdy young men bristling at each other. He'd gotten some bruises and a few scars, nothing more serious. He'd gotten into some fights in prison, but always as a human, and always with the threat of the guards not far away.

This was a no-holds-barred, knock-down, drag-out bear fight. They snarled and tore at each other, slapped at each other with their huge paws, tried to wrestle the other to the ground to sink fangs into his throat. In some distant part of his mind, Gunnar didn't know what he'd actually do if he *did* get Nils down onto the ground. He couldn't see himself killing his brother except perhaps accidentally, in self-defense.

But Nils was giving him no chance to withdraw, no quarter. They roared and tore at each other. Gunnar tasted blood in his mouth, and felt the dragging pain of injuries sapping at him. And yet, there was something freeing about it—when was the last time he'd really been able to let his bear go like this, with no chance of anyone smaller or weaker getting hurt? Their heavy fur was like armor; even their roaring, unleashed bears did relatively little damage to each other.

But he could feel himself starting to tire. Nils was slowing too—but not as quickly. This would be the make-or-break point in the fight, when they both started to make mistakes. This was when a single moment of inattention could be fatal, when the fight might yet drag on for hours or be over in seconds.

With his bear's tunnel vision focused entirely on the fight,

Gunnar hardly registered his surroundings until something huge slammed into both of them, knocking them apart.

Gunnar tumbled into a clump of brush. Panting, confused, he rolled over and pushed himself up on his front legs. Nils—his fur matted with blood, one eye twisted shut—was also picking himself up, growling in fury.

Melody's dragon thumped to the ground, wings outspread and hissing angrily. "What are you doing to my mate?" she demanded. The gold chain on her neck glinted as she tossed her head.

Gunnar shifted so he could talk, wiping blood out of his eyes. Exhaustion and pain hit him hard enough to nearly knock him down again, no longer cushioned by his bear's raw strength and pain tolerance. "Melody, be careful! He's fast." Her dragon was large, compared to a bear, but he was still terrified for her. Could she take on a thousand-pound killing machine, finely honed by training and designed by nature for one purpose only? Melody had the advantage of size, and she had wings, but she was a bookworm who rarely shifted. Fighting was Nils's trade.

Nils seemed to be thinking the same thing. He growled and tensed in what Gunnar recognized as preparation for a charge.

"I'm not afraid of him," Melody declared. "And my father is on his way. If you think you can fight *one* dragon, bear, I'd like to see you take on *two*—ahh!"

As Gunnar had tried to warn her, Nils was fast. But Melody was fast, too. She flowed gracefully aside, using her wings for assistance, and Nils's attempt to snap her slender neck with his paw instead glanced off her scales. One of his claws hooked the chain. It snapped, but not before the locket was crushed against her neck.

Melody's graceful retreat turned into a lurching stumble. Gunnar smelled a sharp, bitter scent that hadn't been there a moment before. Melody was shaking her head as if she was trying to shake something off. Nils looked equally confused, looking down at his paw with the chain tangled in his claws. He shook it to free it of the glittering gold links.

"Melody?" Gunnar said, struggling to his feet. "What's wrong?"

There was really something the matter with her. He thought at first that Nils had hurt her after all, but there was no blood on her silver scales. However, her hindquarters folded and she abruptly sat down, her wings drooping. She raised one forepaw to touch her neck, and then shifted, the great silver dragon-shape collapsing into a small human woman with her fingertips tentatively brushing her throat.

"Melody?" Gunnar said again.

She turned to look at him, her eyes huge and frightened. "Gunnar ..." she said faintly, and then collapsed.

He lurched toward her, forgetting his own pain in his fear. He had no idea what had happened, but *something* clearly had. When he fell to his knees beside her and gathered her into his arms, she was limp and cold to the touch, her breathing fast and shallow.

"What did you do?" he shouted at Nils.

Nils lowered his head and growled. He was readying for another charge. This time Gunnar didn't know how he was going to defend her, defend *them*; he had to shift back, but that meant abandoning Melody, suffering from unknown injuries that had taken her down faster than anything he'd ever seen.

But he couldn't do anything less than go down fighting. He prepared for a shift. Maybe he could wait until the last minute, shift and come up from underneath when Nils charged, and get the drop on him that way—

He didn't even get the chance to try. A dark shadow floated over them, blocking the stars, and a huge dragon crashed to the ground between them, raising a cloud of dust. Gunnar had thought Melody was big, but this dragon dwarfed her. A head as big as a minivan lowered ominously toward Nils, lips drawing back from teeth like a mouthful of swords.

There was no doubt who this was. Darius, Melody had said her father's name was. Right now, Gunnar didn't care if Darius planned to kill him or save him. The important thing was that Melody was dying in his arms, her rapid breathing growing fainter.

"There's something wrong with her!" he cried frantically.

Darius turned his head and inhaled, then jerked back, his nostrils flaring. "Dragonsbane," he rumbled, and turned to look down at Nils, who had flattened his ears and bared his teeth in a snarl. "You. You *dare* attack my daughter, my blood."

And, without waiting for a reply, he pounced.

There wasn't even the slightest chance of Nils's survival, not with a dragon that big and that furious after him. Gunnar cried out helplessly, but there was nothing he could do. He couldn't leave Melody, and anyway, he could see that even two of them together wouldn't have been a match for Darius at the height of his fighting rage; all he could have done was die along with his brother. He couldn't tell if Nils himself realized how badly he was outmatched, even at the end. As far as he could tell, his brother kept fighting right up until the last, when Darius's jaws closed over his neck and ended it with a snap.

Darius flung the body aside and whirled around. As the dragon strode toward Gunnar, who still held Melody in his arms, he shifted in mid-stride: one minute it was the huge gunmetal dragon, the next a tall man with silver-streaked dark hair and sharp, clear eyes that reminded Gunnar of a hawk.

"Wipe that stuff off her," Darius ordered sharply. He tore off his jacket and flung it at Gunnar. "I can't touch her until you do."

Gunnar hadn't even noticed there was anything on her, but liquid glistened in the hollow of her pale throat. He scrubbed at it with Darius's jacket. She was so terribly limp and still, her breathing so shallow—"What's doing this to her? Can you help her?"

"If I can get her back to my estate in time." Darius crouched beside her. "It's concentrated essence of dragons-bane. Lethal to our kind. Where did it come from? Did *you* know of it?"

"I've never heard of it." Gunnar refused to recoil from the menace in Darius's tone. "Whatever it was, she had it inside a necklace." He pointed to the ribbon of moon-touched gold in the churned-up soil. "That."

Darius took a stick and used it to poke at the necklace, as if investigating a venomous snake. He gave Melody another look, and Gunnar glimpsed the veiled anguish on his face. "She was wearing this?"

"Ever since I met her. At least since the first time I saw her with her neck bare." Talking about it helped distract him from Melody's terrible stillness in his arms. He scrubbed vigorously at her neck, wishing he had water. "I thought it was a keepsake."

"It was," Darius murmured, "but not hers." He turned abruptly. "That should be enough. At least, it must be, if I have any hope of saving her. Give her to me."

Gunnar's bear snarled defensively. *Only we can protect our mate!* Human reasoning overruled it; if Melody had any chance, it was with someone who knew what had happened to her and how to fix it. Gunnar carefully transferred her into her father's arms, and for a moment they looked into each other's eyes, steel gray meeting clouded blue. They might not have anything at all in common, but the one thing they did have was the one thing that mattered: they both loved this woman, in their own ways.

"Can you take me with her?" Gunnar asked.

Darius shook his head. "I can fly faster alone. Anyway, that panther son of mine is on your trail. I saw him from the air; he'll be here soon."

With that he shifted, so deftly that Melody's hair hardly stirred as the human arms holding her became a dragon's front legs. Gunnar stepped back as Darius launched himself skyward with a tremendous downbeat of his massive wings.

Gunnar stood watching the dragon dwindle in the night sky. It almost felt as if he could feel his connection to Melody, like a silver chain binding them, stretching as the distance between them grew, but never breaking. Not even death could do that.

Hold on, love. Hold on.

A crashing in the brush announced Ben's arrival. The panther trotted out of the woods and paused, taking in the scene—Nils's body, the torn-up brush and other evidence of the fight, Darius's discarded jacket—with his cool, luminous golden stare before shifting back to his two-legged form. "So," he said laconically. His sharp gaze took in Gunnar's battered condition. "You need a hospital?"

Gunnar shook his head. "I'll heal." Wordlessly, he held out his hands, wrists together.

"And what's that for?"

"Handcuffs."

Ben spread out his arms. He was as naked as Gunnar. "Does it look like I have handcuffs on me?"

Gunnar might have smiled if he hadn't been so worried. If he wanted to escape, he knew, this was his chance. Ben didn't have weapons or a phone, and both his shifted and human forms were smaller than Gunnar's.

But he didn't have the slightest desire to do that. Instead, he crouched beside the broken necklace and picked it up carefully. The bitter smell was stronger this close. Turning it to the minimal light of the sliver-thin moon, he examined the twisted catch of the locket, the smashed pieces of whatever had been inside.

"What's that?" Ben asked, bending over his shoulder. Then he jerked away, coughing.

Gunnar waved him back. "You're part dragon, right? Better not touch this. It's poison to you guys."

Ben bent over, hands on his knees, through a violent coughing fit. "I'll say," he managed at last, stepping back. "That's dragonsbane, isn't it? Wait—" He sucked in a sharp breath and suppressed another cough. "Melody and Dad."

"Melody got it on her," Gunnar said heavily. He stared at the locket, not at Ben. "Your dad took her somewhere. Said he might be able to help her. She was still breathing, last I saw." His voice trailed away.

"If you had anything to do with this ..." The panther's growl underlay Ben's words.

"Not me."

"Your brother?"

Gunnar shook his head. "She had it on her. Melody."

"Wait." Ben sounded thoroughly puzzled. Gunnar looked up. "My sister was carrying around dragonsbane? It's lethal! No dragon would want to come within a mile of that stuff. Why?"

Gunnar lifted his shoulders in a brief shrug. "I don't know. Guess you don't either."

"I have no idea." Ben pointed to the discarded jacket. "Wrap it in that and leave it here. Derek can dispose of it later. With Tessa carrying a part-dragon child, I don't even want to risk getting it on me, let alone anywhere near her."

Gunnar nodded and obeyed. Meanwhile, Ben went over

to inspect Nils's body. "Dad, I'm guessing?" he asked, bending over to examine the wounds.

"Yeah. He was pretty upset about Melody."

"He's not the only one."

The growl was back. Gunnar chose not to point out that Ben's panther probably wouldn't have lasted more than a few minutes against Nils's bear. It didn't matter now.

Nothing mattered, without Melody.

He stayed on his knees, staring at the coat-wrapped bundle, until a hand settled on his shoulder. Startled, he looked up at Ben.

"C'mon. Let's go." Ben prodded at him. "Probably easier to head back if we shift. I don't look forward to a naked hike in the woods, do you?"

"And then what?" It was strangely difficult to care about anything, knowing that Melody hovered on death's doorstep and there wasn't anything he could do about it. His brother was dead; he still couldn't wrap around it, couldn't sort out any of the things he was feeling. "Am I under arrest?"

"Not right now." Ben's voice was gentle. "After we get back to the farmhouse and get cleaned up, I'll take you up to Darius's place. I expect Tessa's going to want to be with Melody, anyway. Derek can handle things here." He glanced at the heap of immobile white fur that had been Nils. "Any requests for what you want done with your brother's body?"

Gunnar shuddered and shook his head.

"Since he died as a bear," Ben said, "there's no way to prove to the authorities that he's actually dead. I guess he'll just remain at large indefinitely. As for the body ... there'll be time to figure that out." He held out a hand. "Let's go."

Gunnar let Ben help him to his feet. Ben shifted, and Gunnar followed suit a moment later, the slim black panther and the big white bear.

If Melody survived, Ben was going to be his brother-in-law. It looked like Ben was starting to come to terms with that.

And if Melody didn't survive ...

Well, in that case, he didn't really care what happened to him, after.

MELODY

There was heat and cold in waves; there was pain, but distant and muffled, as if she was somewhere far away from where her body was. There were voices. She thought she heard her father, and Tessa and Ben. Of the other voice—the one she strained to hear, the one she wanted to hear most—there was no sign.

He'd survived, surely? Fear penetrated her hazy half-awake state, and she struggled to claw her way back to the waking world.

Instead, she clawed her way ... somewhere else.

Melody found herself standing on an endless plain made of fine gray sand that shifted under her slippered feet. The sky was dark, with no stars.

Her dragon sat before her, on its haunches like a dog, silver head upraised and intelligent gray eyes fixed on her.

Melody gazed up at it, awed. She'd never actually seen her dragon before, except from the inside, and its beauty took her breath away. There was grace and power in every clean line of its body, and a predator's cool appraisal in the way its alien eyes studied her.

She'd never quite realized how alien it was before. Other shifters, most of them, shifted into beasts that had real, Earth analogues. They might be larger and more intelligent, but fundamentally they were bears or wolves or dolphins or honey badgers, just like their normal, wild equivalents.

But there was nothing else like dragons on Earth. The only dragons were the shifter kind like Melody and her clan.

For the first time, she thought to wonder, *Where did we come from? Who are we? Are there non-shifter dragons somewhere, under some alien sun?*

Her dragon spoke then, in a musical voice like a pipe organ, somehow different from the way it sounded when her own voice spoke in those fluting tones. It sounded accusing. "You wanted to banish me."

Guilt slapped her in the face: guilt not just for herself and her dragon, but also for Gunnar. "Not you," she protested. "Never you."

"Gunnar then?" her dragon asked.

"No!" she protested. Her gaze dropped to the sand underfoot; she couldn't meet its eyes. "It was me," she said, her voice barely above a whisper. "My fear. My pride. I just wanted a choice."

"And if you could choose now?"

There was a curious timbre to her dragon's voice. She looked up at it.

"Is it true what they say about dragonsbane?" she asked. "Can it break the mate bond?"

"It might. Is that what you want?"

The answer came back to her in the form of memories: Gunnar's sure hands on her body, his warm laugh, the shy way he'd opened up about things he'd never discussed with anyone before. All his courage, his heart, his love, all waiting for her.

"No," she said firmly. "If there *is* a choice, I choose him. Now, today, and every day. Forever."

"Good," her dragon said, sounding pleased.

It settled down on the sand, folding its great legs under it the way Melody had done for Gunnar to mount on her back. She hadn't realized how catlike it looked from the outside. The dragon seemed to be waiting, so Melody went up to it and laid her hand on the silver neck, feeling the pulse of its heartbeat beneath the scales. It felt real. *She* felt real. Nothing else here felt real at all, but *this* was real, she thought.

"I like being able to talk to you like this, face to face," she said, a bit shyly. "I like being able to see more of you than just what I can glimpse out of the corner of my eye."

Her dragon nudged her face with the tip of its great snout, which turned out to be unexpectedly warm and soft. "I *am* you," it said. Its voice was fond and indulgent. "I'm your courage and your secret hidden heart. I'm the fierce part of you and the jealous part of you. I'm the part of you that stands up when everything else falls down."

"Someone's a little full of herself," Melody teased, pushing playfully at the graceful silver neck as she might have shoved her brother when they were children.

Her dragon laughed, a soft laugh for such a huge creature. It was a familiar laugh, Melody realized, because it was her own. "I think you should wake up now. There are others who would like to see you. But remember, I'm part of you. I'll never be farther away than your own soul."

It nuzzled against her face, and then her eyes snapped open, and she woke up.

Her body dragged at her, aching and heavy. She had to blink a few times, trying to clear her vision, and finally raised her hand to her face before she understood that her vision wasn't going to clear; she didn't have her glasses on.

For the first time she realized she hadn't been wearing

them in the dream—or vision, whatever it was. She'd been able to see perfectly clearly without them.

Oh well. I guess dreams don't have to follow real-world logic.

"Melody?" a voice said. A moment later, Tessa's blurry face loomed in her vision. "Melody! You're awake! Can you hear me? Can you sit up?"

Too pliant to offer resistance, Melody let Tessa help her to a sitting position. Her friend fussed around her, propping pillows behind her back and bringing her a glass of water. She didn't have to ask where she was; despite the blurring, she recognized the glitter of gold everywhere and the lush opulence of the bed, which was big enough to accommodate four people. She had to be at Darius's mansion.

A warm, firm lump against her leg settled the matter. It was orange and purring. She didn't have to be able to see it to know it was Toblerone.

"How long was I out?" she asked weakly as Tessa helped her lift the glass of water to her mouth. Her hands trembled and her arms felt limp.

"Two days. We weren't sure—" Tessa pressed her lips together, to stop the words or to prevent them from quivering, Melody wasn't sure. "Anyway," Tessa went on in a more normal voice, "Ben and I have been staying at your father's place while we waited for you to wake up."

It touched her deeply that they'd come. "What about Gunnar?" *He must have survived, he must have. My father was there; I don't remember it well, but I do remember that. Surely he would have made sure that Gunnar survived. He* must *have survived ...*

"He's here," Tessa said, and Melody's stomach unclenched in relief. "Well, not precisely *here* here. Your father wanted him—uh—"

Melody pushed the half-empty glass of water away as her

stomach knit its walls together all over again. "Tessa. Where is Gunnar?"

Tessa cleared her throat. "Did you know your dad has a dungeon? Because I didn't."

"He put him in the *dungeon?*" She started to climb out of bed and immediately got tangled up with the covers and her own weak legs. It was embarrassing to have to slump on Tessa while the spots stopped dancing in front of her eyes.

"I don't think you should be out of bed yet," Tessa protested. "You almost died."

Anger was a remarkable motivator. She managed to wobble to her feet, clutching at Tessa's round, pregnant body for support. "I can't believe my dad put *my mate* in the dungeon. I'm going to kill him."

"In fairness to your dad," Tessa said, putting an arm around her to stabilize her, "Gunnar kind of volunteered to put himself down there. Nobody quite trusts him, and there was some question of—uh—"

"*I* trust him!" Melody snapped. "*I* wanted him here! That should be what counts." She used furniture and Tessa to pull herself toward where she hoped the door was.

"There was some question of how you got the dragons-bane in the first place," Tessa said.

She sounded embarrassed. As well she might. Melody turned a withering glare on her friend, or at least the closest thing she could manage while she was dressed in nothing but a nightgown, unable to see anything except a giant blur, and using her death grip on Tessa's shoulder to keep from falling on her face.

"People think *Gunnar* gave me the dragonsbane?"

"He said he didn't, but I'm not sure your dad and Ben believe him."

"I am going to kill them," Melody decided. "No, first I'll let Gunnar out of the dungeon. Then I'll kill them." She made another attempt for the door, but her human crutch was rooted firmly in place. "Tessa, so help me—"

"I *will* help you, if you'll put some clothes on," Tessa said. "I know how I'd feel if it was Ben down there. At least sit down for a minute, before you fall down."

"I guess ..." Melody wobbled and sat down abruptly on the edge of the bed. "I guess I could do that."

Tessa brought her a silk robe from the closet. "You know they're just trying to look out for you."

"I know," she sighed. "I expect this sort of ridiculousness from Dad. I thought Ben had more common sense, though."

"If it helps any, I think Ben likes Gunnar." Tessa helped Melody put an arm into the robe. "I don't really think he *wants* to, but he does. Ben's always been a pretty good judge of character. Speaking of Ben, he and your dad need to know you're up—"

"They can twist in the wind for a little while yet," Melody declared heartlessly. "First we get Gunnar out of the dungeon. *Then* we let them know I'm not dead."

She almost changed her mind when she lurched out of the bedroom, leaning on Tessa, to be confronted with an expanse of polished marble floor that looked approximately a mile long to her bleary eyes. She'd forgotten how huge Darius's mansion was.

"I'm not quite sure I know the way," Tessa admitted. "This place is a maze."

"I know the way. Just tell me what wing we're in."

"Uh ... he said he put you in the Daffodil Room."

"Really? Okay, that means east wing ..." She turned around. "This way. Onward."

They had to stop a few times along the way to rest, taking shameless advantage of benches that were probably intended to be ornamental. Melody took them down a servant's stair to the basement level, which was older-looking and much more utilitarian than the main floors of the house; it was primarily used for storage. Tessa picked up some self-assurance here, led them through the wine cellar, and opened the secret door to the dungeons with a confidence that indicated she'd already been here a few times.

The women stepped through the swinging section of wall into a square stone passageway. "My father spares no cliché," Melody muttered, glancing at the fuzzy blobs of lamps set into recesses in the rough-cut walls, and Tessa laughed.

Melody just hoped the lamps were electric. Her father was odd and old-fashioned, but he was smart enough not to risk a fire in the subbasement for mere ambiance ... she hoped.

Maddox, her father's bodyguard and manservant, was sitting outside the lone occupied cell in the cell block. He stood up quickly, laying aside a book; Melody had to stop herself from tracking it with her eyes, trying by habit to focus through her nearsightedness to read the cover.

"Melody?" said a familiar, beloved voice, and all thoughts of books fled her mind.

She pushed away from Tessa and stumbled to the bars of the cell. Gunnar scrambled to his feet and pressed against the bars, reaching through. They hugged as desperately as they could with the bars in the way.

"You're all right," Gunnar breathed. He brushed her face with his fingertips before pulling her close again. "You're all right."

"I'm still pretty far from a hundred percent, but I think I'm going to be okay." She pressed against him, as if she could melt through the bars and into his arms. "And you—" She'd already felt the bulk of bandages under his shirt. "Are *you* okay? Are you hurt? They made you stay in here if you're *hurt*—"

"They didn't make me," Gunnar said quickly. "Well, your

BEAR IN A BOOKSHOP

dad kind of ... implied I might be happier here. But it's okay. If you didn't make it, I didn't really ..."

He trailed off. She was glad he hadn't finished. "I'm fine," she declared, "and you're fine. Or at least we're both going to be." She cupped his face in her hands and kissed him.

"Maddox," Tessa said in a no-nonsense tone, "let him out."

"Not without the boss's say-so," Maddox ground back at her in his bass rumble of a voice.

"Maddox, the boss isn't here, but *I'm* here. Which of us are you more worried about?"

Melody was intrigued to find out which way this battle of wills was going to go, but had no chance to learn. "Actually," a quiet voice said from the corridor, "I *am* here." Darius stepped into view, hands clasped behind his back and face calm. If he had any emotional response to the fact that his daughter who had been on her deathbed just recently was now up and moving around, it didn't show—though admittedly she was only getting the broad strokes of expressions right now by squinting at people's faces.

"Daughter," Darius said, and was that perhaps relief in his voice, despite his efforts to hide it? "I see you're up and about."

"Yes, and I see Gunnar is *in the dungeon*," Melody snapped. "Let him out."

Darius nodded to Maddox, who stepped forward with the keys. "Oh, and I brought you something," Darius said casually, holding out a hand to Melody.

She couldn't tell what it was until her hands closed over familiar glass, plastic, and wire. "Oh, thank God," she murmured, fitting the glasses to her face. Finally she could *see*. Darius was smiling slightly. "Where did you get these?"

"I've taken to keeping a spare set on hand, should you need them while visiting."

She'd only started wearing her glasses around him

143

recently; up until that point, they'd both pretended that her eyes were perfectly 20/20. Melody gave him a highly suspicious look, but just then the cell door opened with a clank, and she turned to throw her arms around Gunnar properly this time.

"You're okay," she murmured, pressing kisses to his stubble-scruffed cheek, to his lips and nose and neck.

"I'm okay." He held her close. He must have showered since the fight, because his clothes were clean and he smelled of soap and, ever so slightly, of dungeon.

He could have smelled like a pigpen for all she cared. The important thing was that he was alive and okay. Her conviction from earlier was still with her. *Gunnar, I choose you. No matter what. Through storm and fire, through my family's disapproval, I will always choose you.*

Right now her family was looking uncomfortable and somewhat guilty. Ben had arrived with her dad, and she shot him a glare past Gunnar's shoulder, hoping he could read the unspoken subtext: *I expect this of Dad, but I thought better of you.*

He seemed to understand; there was apology in his slight smile, and then, as he took in the way they were clinging to each other, a long-delayed comprehension seemed to dawn. He went over to put an arm around Tessa's shoulders, and his pregnant mate leaned against him and kissed his cheek.

"I was so worried for you," Gunnar whispered into her hair. "It was all I could think about, how you'd collapsed and I couldn't do anything about it."

"It's all right. It's not your fault in the slightest. No matter what *some people* think." She directed this in Darius's direction.

Darius looked like he was on the verge of saying something, but just then Tessa interrupted them with a small, surprised gasp. She wobbled away from Ben and sat down abruptly on the chair Maddox had vacated.

"Tessa?" Ben said, alarmed.

Darius asked at the same time, "Are you well?"

"I'm fine," Tessa said slowly. She pressed a hand to the swell of her pregnant belly. "I just ... think I had a contraction."

GUNNAR

If there was one thing Gunnar hadn't expected from this day, it was getting caught up in the whirlwind surrounding the delivery of Darius Keegan's first grandchild.

Tessa insisted, at first, on being taken to a hospital—loudly and at length—over the top of Darius's protests that he had excellent medical facilities at the mansion and could have the best doctors brought at once. When Tessa stopped for breath (and another contraction), Ben pointed out that it was a long drive to the nearest hospital, or a slightly less long but considerably more uncomfortable flight on dragonback.

"I'm not due for another two weeks," Tessa protested as they led her upstairs. "Look, there's time to get to a hospital. It's my first child, and I haven't been in labor very long ... I think."

"You *think?*" Melody, Ben, and Darius all said at once.

"Well, I've been having some ... aching, I guess, while I was watching over Melody. I didn't want to say anything because I've been having mild false contractions for weeks, it's a thing that happens—will you two stop looking at me that way," she

146

snapped at Ben and Darius, one of whom was attempting to support her on each side. She shoved Darius away unceremoniously and claimed Ben's hand with her own. "Guys. Do I look like an invalid? Knock it off. I—oh—"

She stopped walking with a groan, and pressed her fist into the small of her back. Ben supported her and gave Darius a desperate look over the top of her head.

"I shall summon a physician," Darius declared, and hurried off.

"I'm not overly comforted by the word 'physician'," Tessa said as Ben helped her to an ornamental bench. "His knowledge of human medicine is more recent than 1890, right? He does know there are medical specialities? Just, I'd rather not have him show up with a proctologist for the delivery of my firstborn."

Melody gave a small laugh. She was leaning on Gunnar, a few steps behind the others, with his arm around her waist to support her. "I don't know how she gets away with it. Nobody can push my father around the way Tessa does. She's got a knack." She glanced up at Gunnar. "I hope the idea of a dragon father-in-law doesn't terrify you."

"I think we've both dealt with worse things than that," he said, leaning down to kiss her.

In the middle of the kiss, they both heard Tessa give a yelp, and Melody broke away and turned to her friend. Ben was looking frantic.

"Tessa, what's wrong?"

Tessa looked up at Ben and Melody with an odd expression on her face, somewhere between embarrassment and satisfaction. "Er ... I think my water just broke on your dad's thousand-dollar bench."

"Good timing," Ben said. He sounded cheerful for the first time in days.

∼

"**D**arius," Tessa said between her teeth, as the white-faced OB/GYN examined the facilities in what appeared to be (to the extent that Gunnar could tell) a modern, state-of-the-art hospital suite in one of the mansion's wings, "when you said *summon* a physician, I wasn't aware *summon* was a code word for *kidnap*."

"No one has been kidnapped," Darius declared, looking slightly more ruffled than usual. "This woman is one of the finest obstetricians in the world, and she owes me a favor. She has been aware for some time that I might cash it in on the delivery of my grandchildren."

"Still, I doubt if she was aware that you might *also* show up in the middle of the night, grab her in your claws, and whisk her off to your secret lair in the mountains."

Darius's eyes narrowed. "She is aware that such things are a hazard of dealing with dragons. And she *does* know about dragons."

"Well, she sure does after one carried her off in the middle of the night!"

"Even before that," Darius said with dignity. "I made sure of it, so that she will be able to handle the situation in case there are unusual complications during the birth."

"Unusual complications?" Tessa's voice rose in a shriek, and she seized Ben's hand in a grip that made him grimace. "This baby is going to come out human-shaped, right? Right? *Darius?*"

"They usually do," Darius said.

"*Usually?!*"

Gunnar grinned and gave Melody a gentle tug, steering her away. "Looks like they've got it handled here. You want to lay down?"

"I'm actually feeling a lot better. The longer I'm up, the

better I feel." She did have more color in her face, Gunnar was relieved to see. "Wait, wait," she went on, pulling away. "I need to find out if Tessa wants anything."

"Go lay down, Mel," was Tessa's answer when Melody asked about it. "I'm fine here. I have Ben, Darius, and all his minions at my beck and call. Go get some sleep. Gunnar, make her go sleep."

"Yes, ma'am," Gunnar said, grinning. This time Melody allowed herself to be shepherded out. "You gonna lay down now?"

"I don't want to," Melody protested. "I'm not that tired. Mostly what I want is food. You?"

"Food sounds great."

"One advantage to Dad being as loaded as he is, all we have to do is call down to the kitchen and they can have whatever we want brought up to our room. What do you want?"

Gunnar's mind went instantly blank. They'd been feeding him in the cell, but the food had tasted like ashes while he didn't know if Melody was going to be all right. Now he realized he was starving. "Uh ... burger?"

"We can do better than that. How about the biggest, juiciest, rarest rib-eye you've ever seen?"

His mouth watered. "Make it two and you've got a deal."

Not long after, they had a meal fit for a king—or at least a wealthy dragon—spread over the yellow-and-white bedspread in what Melody told him was called the Daffodil Room. "All the guest bedrooms have a theme," Melody explained. "If the yellow bothers you, we can move over to Pine or Sage or Bluebell."

"This is fine. It's cheerful." He looked around at the cream-colored carpet, the furnishings that looked like they probably came from fancy lines of furniture with fancy furniture-style names, and the door standing open to a bathroom with a huge Jacuzzi and an expanse of white-and-yellow tiled floor. "This is like some kind of fancy hotel, more than a house."

"We could sleep in a different room every night, if you want to. I used to enjoy doing that when I'd visit Dad as a kid."

Gunnar flushed and shook his head. "I wouldn't want to. It feels like ... too much, you know? I don't need it. This one room is nicer than anywhere I've ever been. Anyway, no sense making somebody have to change the sheets on all those beds and clean all those rooms if we don't need to."

Melody's eyebrows went up, and she thoughtfully forked up a piece of triple-layer chocolate cake with little chocolate curls on top. In addition to the steaks, she'd had the kitchen send up what looked to Gunnar like some of everything; there was more food than even a couple of healing shifters could eat. "I never thought about it that way before," she said.

"You mop enough floors, you can't help thinking about the people that mop the floors, even in a place like this. I mean, someone's gotta polish all that marble out there."

Her face lit up in a smile, and she reached out to curl her fingers over his wrist. "Gunnar, you're not only a good person, I think you're the best person I've ever known."

"I'm not," he protested, looking away.

Her fingers remained on his wrist, pressed gently like a benediction. "You are, though. Everything you've been through, everything with your brother and the life you've led —it could have made you hard and cold. It could have made you like Nils. But all it did was make you kind. You don't want other people to be hurt the way you were hurt."

She found his lips with hers, and for awhile the food was forgotten in gentle kissing and nibbling, relearning the shape of each other's mouths.

Eventually they came up for air, and more dessert. In

between feeding each other chocolate-covered strawberries, Melody asked hesitantly, "Do you mind if I ask about your, um, legal situation? Do you know what's going to happen to you now that Nils is—um—now that he's no longer—"

"You can say dead," Gunnar said gently. It seemed to him that it should hurt more than it did, but when he prodded at thoughts of his brother as if probing a healing injury, all he found was a sad, resigned grief, not the acute pain he'd feared. "I talked to your brother a little bit while I was in the, er ..."

"You can say dungeon." Anger flashed across her face. "I still can't believe they did that. I am definitely having a little word with my dad about that. I'll have the stupid thing bricked up if I have to."

"I didn't mind it. Really. But anyway, your brother and I talked about it, and he'll be working on getting me a full release. Your dad can afford some pretty good lawyers."

"I guess his money might as well be good for something," Melody said grudgingly.

Gunnar kissed the corner of her mouth. "Do you really want to sit here and talk about your dad?"

"Not really ..."

They kissed some more, not just on the lips; he nibbled down the soft skin of her neck, and she kissed his shoulders and collarbone, taking care with the fresh purplish scars where his fast shifter healing was still dealing with his injuries from the fight with Nils. He slipped her robe down from her pale shoulders and then took off her glasses gently, setting them on the nightstand. "I haven't gotten a close look at your eyes without these," he murmured.

"They're just eyes," she said, her voice a whisper with a smile in it.

"Nothing about you is 'just' anything to me."

She blinked up at him, and he decided her eyes were

beautiful behind her glasses, and just as beautiful without. He bore her down to the bed, and they ended up getting chocolate in her hair and having to wash it out later, but it was worth it.

~

As they lay in each other's arms, damp from a leisurely dip in the enormous tub in the bathroom, Melody murmured, "You haven't asked about the dragonsbane."

"I didn't think it was any of my business," Gunnar said quietly.

"No, but I don't want any secrets between us. Not anymore." She propped herself up on her elbow, beautiful and unselfconscious in her soft, curvaceous nakedness. "I've been carrying around dragonsbane with me for awhile. I, um, borrowed it from Dad awhile back, without his knowledge."

"Were you ..." Gunnar hesitated. "Were you planning to ... hurt yourself? Or someone else?"

"No!" she said quickly. "No, not at all. No, it was a ... hope, a foolish hope, back when all of this first started, that I could use the dragonsbane to get control over the mate bond between us. I think maybe I knew all along that it wouldn't work. But it took me awhile to give in, to just let go and feel what I didn't want to admit I was feeling." She grimaced. "To be honest, I got so used to carrying it around with me that I forgot I had it. I'm just glad nobody else got hurt, like Ben or, God forbid, Tessa or the baby. If nothing else, I guess I've learned to be more careful."

"With deadly poisons? Good to hear."

Melody let out a soft sigh, and settled with her head in the crook of his shoulder. He stroked her bare arm gently, reassuring himself that she was here with him, each soft breath a reminder that she was okay. "Are you feeling better?" he asked quietly.

"I'm feeling pretty much back to normal, honestly. And a little bit stupid. And definitely determined not to do anything like that again." After a little while, she asked, "What about you? How are *you* doing?"

He didn't pretend that he didn't know what she meant. "Okay, I guess. I had a lot of time to think about Nils while I was locked up in the ... basement."

Melody growled under her breath. Gunnar kissed her cheek gently.

"Don't blame them too much for it. Having the time to myself was good for me, and it gave me time to think it over. To work things out in my own head. I lost my brother a long time ago; I just didn't want to admit it."

"I'm sorry," Melody whispered. "I thought I knew what it's like when your family isn't what you want them to be, but it's not at all the same for me. My family, however frustrating they are, always has my back. Yours ..."

"It's the past. We can't change it. All we can do is make our own future." He kissed the top of her head. "And I have you, now."

"Always," she whispered into his shoulder. "You'll always have me. No matter what."

MELODY

They were lying together, skin to skin, half asleep, when there was a brisk knock on the door. "Hey, Melody," Ben called through the door. "Want to come meet your new baby niece?"

Melody sat bolt upright in bed, stark naked, her hair a tangled mess hanging in her face. "Coming!" she called, and then, hastily, "Don't come in!"

There was a soft laugh from the other side of the door. "Not planning on it."

Melody stretched and swung her legs off the bed. "C'mon." She prodded at Gunnar. "Get dressed."

"You sure I'll be welcome? This is a family thing."

"And you're family," Melody declared. "Mine. If anyone has a problem with it, they can take it up with me. Put some pants on and let's go."

She found clothes that fit her in the dresser, and decided not to wonder where they'd come from—if Tessa brought them, or if her father had taken to keeping spare clothes of hers on hand. She didn't recognize them, but they were in her general style, a soft kitten-gray sweater and gray slacks with a glossy pearlescent sheen. Both looked expensive. *Probably Dad, then.*

She expected to find Ben out in the hall—either that or to find the hall empty, Ben having gone back to Tessa and the baby. What she was not expecting was her dad, leaning on the wall, looking well put together and slightly bored in that typical Darius sort of way.

"Where's Ben?" Melody asked.

"He's gone to be with his mate. I, on the other hand," Darius said, "have been thrown out of the delivery room, unceremoniously thrown out in my own house."

"I truly can't imagine why," Melody said, tucking her fingers into Gunnar's hand. "So what does it feel like to be a grandpa?"

"I'm sure I'll survive it," Darius said mildly, the corner of his mouth twitching as if to suppress a smile. He raised an eyebrow at both of them. "And what is the prognosis of grandchildren coming from this direction anytime soon?"

"None of your business, that's what," Melody said primly, while Gunnar blushed.

The mansion's medical wing had changed utterly since Melody had last been there some twelve or so hours earlier. Now there were dim lights, candles, and music playing softly. Clearly Tessa had taken full advantage of having minions at her beck and call to do some redecorating.

Tessa herself was lying on a bed in a pile of blankets, with the baby bundled up in a soft pale-yellow blanket and resting on her chest. She looked exhausted but euphoric. Ben was next to her, holding her hand and looking quietly delighted. He kept looking down at the blanket-wrapped baby as if he couldn't quite believe it was real. Darius hung back discreetly in the doorway.

"I'm sorry I wasn't there for the birth," Melody said, hugging her friend carefully around the baby.

"I'm not," Tessa said, hugging her back. "The last thing I wanted was a bunch of other people underfoot, trust me. Ben and the OB/GYN were about all the company I could handle. Do you want to hold her?"

"I—um—maybe?" Melody said blankly, as Tessa put the little blanket-wrapped bundle into her arms. She hadn't realized newborn babies were so shockingly tiny. The baby weighed almost nothing. Her little red face was scrunched up and she had dark curls plastered to her tiny head.

Melody had never thought of herself as a person who was into babies. Only now, looking down at the tiny, fragile little newborn person in her arms, she found herself falling completely and utterly in love.

"What's her name?" Gunnar asked quietly. He'd stepped closer and was looking down at the baby with a soft, captivated expression that went deep into Melody's chest. What would his face look like, looking at a child of his own? She wanted, suddenly, to find out.

"We haven't quite decided yet," Tessa said. "We've known it was a girl for a few months; we just didn't tell anyone. I figured by now we'd have a name picked out, but ..."

"Do you have a list?" Melody asked, glancing up from the baby she was still shyly cradling.

"Sure we do, but it's fifteen names long."

"Darius is an excellent name," Darius said, from the doorway.

"Not for a girl, thank you."

"Daria, then. Very strong name, very traditional."

"She doesn't need a strong name, Dad, she's maybe two pounds at most," Melody said, looking down again at the tiny person in her arms.

"Six pounds, ten ounces," Ben said.

She weighed less than a gallon-sized carton of milk, Melody thought. She would fit *inside* a carton of milk.

"All the more reason to need a strong name," Darius said, unruffled. He turned at a discreet tap on his shoulder from Maddox, and the two men spoke quietly for a moment. "Ah, we've a guest."

"A guest?" Tessa said, sitting up in bed from where she'd been wilting sleepily on Ben's shoulder. "A guest, *in here*? I *hope* you don't mean in here, Darius."

"It's been some time, my Heart," said Heikon, bowing his way into the room.

Ben scrambled to his feet and put himself protectively between Tessa and the rival dragon clanlord. Melody could sense his panther near the surface. Her dragon was bristling as well.

"My mate just had a baby, Heikon," Ben said between his teeth. "I don't know if Dad called you, or if you just decided to show up, but you're not welcome here. Tessa isn't yours anymore, to the extent she ever was."

"I'm only here for a moment." Heikon reached up to touch something on his shoulder, and Melody nearly jumped as a very small dragon uncoiled from around his neck. The little dragon was jewel-green, with glimmering green and copper wings, and there was something sparkly tangled up in its claws. "I'm told you have a baby girl. Where is she?"

"Uh, she's here," Melody said, curling protectively around the baby in her arms, "but I don't think her parents want you to hold her."

"I wasn't going to ask, and I won't be long." Heikon's glance at Tessa was fond and amused, even though Tessa looked like she wanted to strangle him. "Her family served mine faithfully for many years, and I promised a gift to her firstborn. It's okay, Feodran," he coaxed the little dragon, holding it against his chest. "Go ahead and shift."

The little dragon shifted suddenly into a small, cute child, with dark ringlets and large brown eyes. After looking quickly around at all the adults staring at him, the little boy turned his face shyly against Heikon's chest.

"You can give it to her," Heikon said, his voice soft and gentle. "She's here."

He brought the little boy to Melody, who frowned in puzzlement, but didn't back away. "This is my great-grandson, Feodran," Heikon explained. "Feodran, give Tessa's daughter what you brought her."

The little boy shyly unclenched his chubby fists and dropped a glittering gold chain onto the blanket-wrapped bundle in Melody's arms. A green stone winked up at her from the pale yellow blanket, embedded in a setting encrusted with—

"Are those *diamonds*?" Melody asked.

"Is that a real emerald?" Tessa said.

"She's two hours old, Heikon." Ben sounded somewhere between amusement and exasperation. "At least wait until she opens her eyes before showering her with priceless treasures."

"The jewel is merely a symbol," Heikon explained. "With this offering from our family hoard, our children are bonded in future betrothal, the greatest honor my clan can bestow. This child will be the woman you'll marry someday, Feodran."

There was a dead silence, then Tessa said, "Are you *high*? The gift you said you were going to give my baby is an *arranged marriage*?"

"It's traditional," Darius spoke up. "And it's a tremendous honor, particularly given your child's ..." He glanced at Ben. "... unusual pedigree. We don't even know if she'll be a dragon. Truly, it is a surprising act of good faith on the Corcorans' part."

"Whoa." Ben caught his mate as she started to climb out of bed, fists clenched, looking fully prepared to take on both the dragon clanlords who were now eyeing her with wary bemusement. "Settle down, honey. This isn't happening. You got that, Heikon? No way. We're not betrothing our daughter to someone else's kid before she can even walk."

"Damn straight we're not!" Tessa snarled. "This is the 21st century, not the Middle Ages! Darius, we are having *words*!"

Feodran whimpered and pressed his face into Heikon's chest. "Now you've upset the child," Heikon said.

"You're the one who dragged the child here!" Tessa said, but she softened and patted Feodran's back. "It's okay, sweetie, no one's mad at you. It's very sweet of you to give my daughter a gift. It's a very nice necklace and I'm sure she'll love it ... once she's old enough not to eat it," she muttered under her breath.

"As for you, Dad ..." Ben growled through his teeth as he gently steered his mate back to bed. "I can't believe you knew about this and agreed. Well, okay, I *can* believe it—"

"It's not as if it's the first time he's done this," Melody said. Everyone looked at her. "What? Dad tried to betroth me, too, when I was just a little older than this."

"Wait, he did *what*?" Ben said.

"Betrothed me. As I recall, it was to the son of the Lachlan clanlord, wasn't it, Dad? Who was fifteen years older than me, and, as I recall, turned out to be gay anyway."

"My intentions were good," Darius said stiffly. "It would have worked out if either of you had tried to make it work."

"Dad. He's gay. And also at least fifty by now."

"So? We can live for hundreds of years! What's a decade or two, counted against that?"

"What about fated mates?" Gunnar asked. He'd been

hovering near Melody, staying out of the fight as much as possible, but she was aware of his solid strength against her back, there to back her up if needed. "You can't just decide who your kids are going to marry. It doesn't work that way for us—for shifters."

"Hmph," Darius said. "Fated mates. Fated *nonsense*, is what it is. Dragons aren't as concerned about such things as lesser shifters. I wasn't mated to the mothers of either of my children."

"Yeah, and how'd that work out for you, Dad?" Ben said in a tone that indicated his patience was fraying to its snapping point.

"I'll just leave you lot to this, shall I?" Heikon said quickly, tucking Feodran firmly against his chest. "It's past this one's bedtime." Leaning close to the baby in Melody's arms, he murmured, "Enjoy your necklace, little one. We'll talk about the rest of it when you're older."

"No you won't!" Tessa declared, struggling to get up again while Ben held her back. "There are no arranged marriages happening in this family, at least not in *my* part of this family. Darius! I'm going to strangle you!"

"I'll just walk you out, Heikon," Darius declared, and he and Heikon swiftly vanished.

"I'm gonna kill him," Tessa said conversationally. "If not today, then eventually. I'm going to stab that man to death with a tiny oyster fork in the middle of an uncomfortable family dinner someday. Melody, may I have my daughter back, please?"

"Uh, sure." The baby had been sleeping quietly in Melody's arms, seeming undisturbed by the quarrel going on around her. Melody carefully deposited her back on Tessa's chest. "What do you want to do with, um ..." She held up the necklace. Those were *definitely* real diamonds.

"I guess it'll be a good start to her college savings fund,"

Ben said, with a sigh. "I don't suppose you could put it in Dad's safe for me?"

"I'd be happy to." Melody folded it up in her palm. Although she didn't feel the covetous urge for sparkly things in the way some dragons did, there was something very satisfying about holding the gold and jewels, if only for a few minutes. "Is there anything else you two need? Er, you three, I mean."

"A restraining order to keep Darius a hundred yards away from me at all times," Tessa said grimly, and then yawned. Her eyelids were starting to flutter shut.

"He'll stay out of this room for awhile if he knows what's good for him," Ben said. "He has to take the doc home, anyway."

Melody gave her sister-in-law another hug, then Ben, and Ben and Gunnar shook hands. "Congratulations, man," Gunnar said. "I don't know much about babies, but she's real cute."

Melody and Gunnar left, hand in hand. "Were they serious?" Gunnar asked. "About the arranged marriage."

"I'm afraid so. Luckily, my dad does roll with modern times, in his own way, even if he won't admit it. Give him a little while, and he'll probably have convinced himself that breaking the betrothal was his idea, and pat himself on the back for how modern he is."

She let herself into her father's office, and then discovered that the safe no longer responded to the code she used to use. She tried the other passcodes that she knew of her father's, and none of them worked either. If she had been able to open it, she was willing to bet she would have discovered the little case with the dragonsbane had been moved somewhere else.

"Can't get it open?" Gunnar asked.

"No. I guess he changed the code." She placed the necklace carefully on her father's desk.

"I might be able to crack that safe for you."

"Thank you for the offer, but there's no need. It'll be perfectly safe here. No one is going to steal it from the depths of a dragon's lair."

"What if your dad mistakes it for one of his?"

"He won't. Dragons know every piece of their hoard by sight, trust me. He'll know what it is, and he'll keep it safe for her until she's older."

"You trust your dad that much?" Gunnar asked as they turned away, leaving the office to its shadows.

"It's not a matter of trust; it's a matter of honor. My dad has his flaws, boy does he ever, but if it has to do with his honor, you can trust him a hundred percent. He wouldn't steal his granddaughter's dowry."

Gunnar was quiet and contemplative as she locked the office door again. "Are you all right?" Melody asked him. "Is it about your brother?"

"No. Like I said earlier, Nils made his choices, most of them a long time ago. No ..." He gave his head a brief shake. "It's not Nils. I was actually thinking about something your dad said earlier, about dragons living for hundreds of years. Are *you* going to live for hundreds of years?"

She immediately understood why that was bothering him. "And you're afraid you won't?"

"I know I won't," Gunnar said. "Unless you know something about me that I don't know."

"It doesn't quite work like that." Melody chewed her bottom lip. "From what Mom told me, your lifespan adjusts itself to your mate's. I think that means you'll live longer than most bear shifters, and I won't live quite as long as an unmated dragon would. But that's okay. I don't want to be two hundred years old anyway. I just want to live out a normal lifespan with you, and watch our kids grow up and have kids of their own."

"Kids?" he asked quietly, taking her hand.

"If you want them," she said quickly.

Gunnar leaned in to take her lips in a gentle kiss, and then rested his forehead against hers. "I want whatever you want," he murmured. "Whatever makes you happy. Forever."

EPILOGUE

"*A Complete World History of Twine,*" Gunnar read carefully off the flaking spine of the hardbound book. "Really? We're keeping this one?"

"Someone might want to know all about twine," Melody said quickly. "And then where will we be? Completely out of books about twine, that's where."

They were both sitting on the floor of what had been, until recently, Hidden Treasures Used Books. Now it was a disorganized space full of heaps of books, cardboard boxes, and half-empty shelves. The door had a CLOSED AND MOVING sign hanging from it, but it stood half open to let in the afternoon sunshine.

"I can't help noticing we aren't putting very many books in the donation box," Gunnar said. "You know we don't have space for even half of these."

"I know, but Gaby's already said she and Derek will store everything we're not taking at the farmhouse. They have plenty of room there. There's no need to get rid of anything at all."

Gunnar rolled his eyes affectionately. "We're going to

have to buy a house the size of your dad's mansion to store all our books, aren't we?"

"Maybe just a storage unit." Melody cleared her throat and put two more books in the box beside her knee, labeled POETRY H-M in black marker. The DONATION box was still empty except for a very scuffed copy of *The Little Engine That Could*, and that only because Gunnar had pointed out they already had two copies in much better shape.

"A storage unit the size of a warehouse, maybe," Gunnar teased.

Melody grinned and poked him in the leg with her toe. He caught her ankle and rubbed his thumb above the hollow of her heel, just above the top of her sensible shoe.

"Gunnar," she protested, making no move to escape. "We have to get these books boxed up and sort out the ones we're taking with us."

"You *sure* that sorting books is all you feel like doing today?"

Her foot twitched in his gentle grip. "Absolutely," she declared. "Book sorting and nothing else."

Gunnar massaged her ankle and grinned as her eyes half-closed in bliss.

"I could come back later if I'm interrupting something." Tessa's cheerful voice came from the doorway, as her shadow fell across the book piles and half-packed boxes.

"We're just sorting books," Melody said quickly, attempting to pull her foot back. Gunnar hung on, grinning at her.

Tessa came in. She had her daughter in a front carrier; a tuft of the baby's dark hair was visible, nestled against her chest. "Brought you two lunch from Gaby's café," she said, holding up a paper bag. "Sandwiches and some of her world-famous bear claws."

"Oh, yum." Melody took custody of the bag. "Thank you."

"Hey, there's a price. No free lunch in this world. I also came over to see the RV," Tessa went on brightly. "Gaby told me you finished the last of the interior work, and you had it here at the bookstore today so you could load it up. I didn't see it out front, though."

"No, it's behind the store, in the alley." Melody gave her foot a gentle twist, and Gunnar regretfully let go so she could hop to her feet. "I'll show you. Hon, could you bring a box since we're going that way?"

"Does it matter which one?"

"No, not really—Not that one!" He'd started to pick up the box of poetry books she'd been working on. "That's not full yet. Take the ... um ... how about that box of mysteries there. We still need to fill up those shelves."

Gunnar shared a fondly commiserating look with Tessa and picked up the box effortlessly in his strong arms. Carrying another box with the lunch bag balanced on top, Melody led the way—at least until she was confronted with the need to open the door leading back to the alley. Tessa hurried forward to open it for her.

The alley behind the row of businesses along Main Street was actually more of a gravel parking area, easily wide enough to accommodate a recently remodeled and repainted motor home. For the last few weeks, ever since Melody had bought it, the RV had been parked at Gaby and Derek's farm, taking advantage of the farm's workshop and Ben and Derek's combined woodworking expertise (which Gunnar had been picking up with a flair). Melody had thrown herself into every aspect of the RV's makeover, from providing the basic designs to cutting shelves to long hours painstakingly painting the exterior.

And now it was done. Where there had been a beige, ordinary-looking motor home, now there was a brightly painted vehicle that declared in bold letters on the side: HIDDEN TREASURES TRAVELING BOOKSTORE.

"Hang on, I'll just pop the sides out so you can see the whole thing," Melody said, dropping her box next to the door and hopping up inside.

Tessa poked her head in after her friend. "You're really going to have room for both of you in here *and* a bunch of books?"

"It'll be a little cramped," Melody admitted. "But we'll have the whole great outdoors for camping, too. I've never camped out, and Gunnar says he's always wanted to. We've kept the bathroom and kitchen, and some fold-out sleeping space inside. And everything else," she declared with a flourish, "is bookshelves."

With the RV's pop-out sides opened up, there was a surprising amount of bookshelf space. Tessa oohed and ahhed over it, and admired the little fold-down wooden bars that Ben and Derek had rigged on each shelf; they kept the books clamped firmly in place while the RV was moving, and could be moved down, out of the way, when it was parked.

There were also some very special shelves, separate from the others, for the books Melody didn't intend to sell. These shelves currently held Melody's forty or fifty most important books (cut down, with great agonizing, from her several hundred most important books) and, just as important, the small but growing collection of Gunnar's books, including *The Story of Ferdinand* and some workbooks for dyslexic students that they'd been working on together.

"With this, we'll be able to take our bookstore to towns across the country," Melody said, briskly shelving books from the mystery-novel box as she talked. "Towns that are too small to have ever had their own bookstore, and towns that used to have one that closed. We can go to farms and ranches and schools, nursing homes, Walmart parking lots—

and big cities too, inner-city neighborhoods that don't have any bookstores, local fairs and festivals ... I can't *wait*."

"I'm really impressed," Tessa remarked, handing books to Melody to be shelved. "Some couples might've had a conflict if one wanted to travel and the other wanted to run a bookstore. You two just found a compromise."

"It certainly helps that I don't mind traveling too, as long as I've got my books. If Mom can travel with her music hoard on a digital player, why can't I take my books with me too?"

Tessa coughed something into her hand that sounded like "*ebook reader*."

"Hey! One small step at a time! I do have an ebook reader ... well, a few of them, actually ..."

"I know you have at least one, since it was what I gave you for Christmas last year."

"Oh hush. The point is ... baby steps." She inhaled deeply of the book smell mixed with the sharpness of newly finished wood from the just-installed bookshelves. "I'm a dragon. I need to be able to curl up with my hoard around me."

"Just your hoard?" Tessa asked, smiling, and both of them looked through the window of the RV at Gunnar, shoulders flexing under his T-shirt as he lowered another box of books to the stack outside the bookstore's back door.

"Okay, yes, I like to curl up with more than just books." Melody could feel her cheeks turning pink. "And sometimes we curl up and read books *together*. In bed."

"That definitely sounds like your idea of a perfect evening."

Melody cleared her throat and slipped another book into its slot on the shelf. "The *point* is, maybe someday an ebook reader will be enough for me, but for now, I have my traveling hoard and I have my mate, and that *is* enough." And Gunnar *could* travel; that was the best part. They'd finally gotten the legal paperwork cleared up, and he was a free man.

"I'm glad you're happy." Tessa hugged her friend, swinging the baby carrier to the side to avoid squishing the baby between them. "You'll have to write, of course. Send post-cards. And *definitely* tell me when Ben and I can expect a new little niece or nephew."

"One thing at a time. You'll just have to deal with being Aunt Tessa to Gaby and Derek's kids for now, not to mention Mom to your own." Melody kissed the top of the baby's soft little head. "But you'll be the first to know, I promise."

"Are you coming back to the farm tonight?"

"Not sure," Melody said. "Any specific reason?"

"Just hoping we'll get to say goodbye before you leave."

Melody had to laugh. "We're not skipping town without saying goodbye, don't worry. I mean, look at all of this. We've still got a ways to go before we're ready to leave."

Later in the afternoon, Tessa was long gone back to the cabin up in the hills that she shared with Ben, and Melody walked around the now-echoing bookstore, retrieving books from dusty corners where they'd slipped down behind shelves or gotten kicked under chairs. She took down a notice for a music act that had played at the biker bar months ago.

They weren't quite done packing up the bookstore. There was still some work to go—a couple of days, at least, before it was empty and clean and awaiting its next tenants. But she'd already moved out in her head and her heart. Most of the books were safely tucked away in the RV or boxed to be moved to Derek and Gaby's farm, and she was already fantasizing about getting on the road.

"Penny for your thoughts." Gunnar slipped an arm around her from behind, and Melody sighed and leaned back against him.

"Just looking forward to our future. By the way, I think Tessa is planning on throwing a going-away party for us, just to warn you."

"What did she say?"

"It's not what she said, it's that the subtle hints are getting less subtle. She and Gaby have had their heads together a lot."

"At least if Gaby's involved, we know the food will be good." He nuzzled against her neck. "Once we get on the road, any thoughts on where we should go first?"

She turned her head to give him better access, smiling. Little shivers ran through her from her toes to the top of her head as he nuzzled at her nape. "What do you think about the seacoast?"

"You want to see the ocean?" he asked, kissing the side of her neck.

She tilted her head back to look up at him. "I've seen it already, though I'd like to see it again, but more than anything else, I want *you* to see the ocean. I think your bear deserves a chance to swim in real ocean waters, somewhere you don't have to worry about being seen ... don't you?"

His face was startled and open for a moment. He still wasn't used to people thinking about his feelings or taking his needs into account. Well ... she would just have to change that.

"Yeah," he said quietly. "Yeah ... I think I'd like that a lot."

A vision popped into her head of Gunnar shedding his clothes and slipping into the water at a deserted stretch of beach, with the setting sun turning his skin to gold. Melody smiled and turned around in his arms so she could lace her own arms around his neck. "Of course I might have a very tiny ulterior motive or two," she murmured against his lips.

"Seeing how it's such a hardship watching you take your clothes off."

"A hardship, is it," he murmured, unbuttoning the top two buttons of her sensible blouse.

"Hmm. I think perhaps I should shut the door."

A little while later, they were lying on the floor, amid scattered books and discarded clothing, in a shaft of late-afternoon sun slanting through the window. "You know," Gunnar murmured, stroking her hair, "I think I'm going to miss this place. Or at least the good memories."

"We just need to make sure the new tenants don't find out what we've been doing on their floor. Or how many times we've done it."

Gunnar laughed softly and buried his face in her hair, and she curled into him, filled with a deep warm sense of relaxation and fulfillment. It was a satisfaction both internal and external, the physical release of good sex and the emotional wholeness of having her mate's arms around her, feeling her mate's breath against her skin.

Home, she now knew, wasn't a place. Home was in Gunnar's arms. Home was having love all around her and a few good books with her (and, okay, knowing the rest of her books were safely stored with Gaby; friends were a treasure, too).

Wherever they went, she thought, it didn't really matter, though she was looking forward to it. They could travel, or settle down; it would all be okay. Everything she wanted, everything she needed was right here with her.

I f you enjoyed this book, you can join my mailing list to read a free sequel story about Melody and Gunnar and their traveling bookshop! And you can make sure not to miss another book, in this or any of my other series.

http://www.zoechant.com/join-my-mailing-list/

There is also a convenient boxed set of the first four books available.

A NOTE FROM ZOE CHANT

Thank you for buying my book! I hope you enjoyed it. If you'd like to be emailed when I release my next book, please click here to be added to my mailing list: http://www.zoechant.com/join-my-mailing-list/. You can also visit my webpage at zoechant.com or follow me on Facebook or Twitter. You are also invited to join my VIP Readers Group on Facebook!

Please consider reviewing *Bear in a Bookshop*, even if you only write a line or two. I appreciate all reviews, whether positive or negative.

If you liked this book, there is a convenient boxed set of the first four books in the series. Please see the next page for a list of all the books in the series and links to their Amazon pages!

Cover art: © Depositphoto.com

ALSO BY ZOE CHANT

Stone Shifters

Stoneskin Dragon

Stonewing Guardian

Stoneheart Lion (forthcoming)

Bodyguard Shifters

Bearista

Pet Rescue Panther

Bear in a Bookshop

Day Care Dragon

Bull in a Tea Shop

Dancer Dragon

Babysitter Bear

There is a convenient boxed set of the first four books.

Bears of Pinerock County

Sheriff Bear

Bad Boy Bear

Alpha Rancher Bear

Mountain Guardian Bear

Hired Bear

A Pinerock Christmas

Boxed Set #1 (collects Books 1-3)

Boxed Set #2 (collects Books 4-6)

And more ... see my website for a full list at zoechant.com!

~

If you enjoyed this book, you might also like my paranormal romance and sci-fi romance written as Lauren Esker!

Shifter Agents

Handcuffed to the Bear

Guard Wolf

Dragon's Luck

Tiger in the Hot Zone

Shifter Agents Boxed Set #1

(Collecting *Handcuffed to the Bear, Guard Wolf,* and *Dragon's Luck)*

Standalone Paranormal Romance

Wolf in Sheep's Clothing

Keeping Her Pride

Warriors of Galatea

Metal Wolf

Metal Dragon

Metal Pirate